THUNDER

LIGHTNING HOPKINS BOOK 3

KEITH SOARES

CONTENTS

PART III
A TURN FROM THE SUN

Bufflegoat Books LLC
First print edition November 25, 2020
ISBN 978-1-7342349-7-8
Original publication date November 25, 2020

Cover Photography: Dave Scavone, Scavone Photography
Model: Stephanie Japec
Other images licensed from iStock by Getty Images

**Dedicated to the twelve year void that
can't be filled simply by searching the world.**

ALSO FROM KEITH SOARES

The Oasis of Filth

Part 1 - The Oasis of Filth

Part 2 - The Hopeless Pastures

Part 3 - From Blood Reborn

—

The Fingers of the Colossus (Ten Short Stories)

—

John Black

For I Could Lift My Finger and Black Out the Sun

If Only Every Moment Was Black and White

And It Arose From the Deepest Black

The Night Is Black, Without a Moon

On a Black Wind Blows Doom

The Black Eye of the Beholder

In the Black Veins of the Earth

Cloak of Black, Mantle of Sorrow

—

Lightning Hopkins

Struck

Twice

Thunder

NEWSLETTER

Sign Up for Keith Soares's New Releases Newsletter

Get release news and free books, including private giveaways and preview chapters. To join, just visit KeithSoares.com and select the option at the top of the page to get two free books, or go directly to the newsletter sign up form.

facebook.com/KeithSoaresAuthor
twitter.com/ksoares

PREFACE

Alexandria, Virginia
October 20, 2020

We're all charge hunting, in our own way. Trying to find something that fills us up with the energy and drive to go again. Not a goal in itself, but the gas station pit stop on the road to life's goals.

Yet, just like filling a car with gas, sometimes that fuel gets used up and you didn't really go anywhere with it, you more or less just did loose circles and came back to the same place.

As I'm writing this preface, and as has been the case for the duration of writing this book, the world is in the midst of a global pandemic. Now every journey feels like loose circles leading back to the same place. Like a lot of people, I had plans for this year, and some of those plans involved visiting far off places. None happened, and I'm not completely sure when such things might happen again.

I began 2020 with the plan of writing full time for the first time in my life. I expected to have an empty house and hours of freedom to create. Life had other ideas, and instead, every day the house is full of people, each on their own weird schedule of wake, eat, video conference, eat, sleep. We've attained an equilibrium with it, but it wasn't what any of us expected.

It took a while to find a new way forward with creativity, but what I discovered was that spending time in another world was a healthy diversion for me. I hope that you, too, can enjoy spending time in Lyn Hopkins's world, and I hope that as she travels the globe on her own strange journey, you can find a sliver of the past and, more importantly, of the future. Places in time where traveling to Switzerland, France, or Venezuela aren't just make believe.

Keith Soares
keith@keithsoares.com

PART I

A WOE THAT IS MADNESS

1

NOTHING WILL CHANGE MY MIND, EXCEPT THAT

"*B*onsoir, mademoiselle."

I stare out over the calm waters of the lake as a fluffy duckling waddles past me, seemingly without a care in the world. Asphalt and stone end just feet from my chair, and the little bird pauses at the edge with a brief flutter of its wings like some high diver stretching in preparation. Paddling nearby, its mother circles her brood, four or five bright yellow bobbing dots contrasting with the cool blue of the rippling waves. The mother quacks once, a prompt for her straggling child, and the duckling echoes her with a thin, frail response before hopping off the stone and splashing into the water.

A little family reunion, I think, mentally grumbling but keenly aware that I'm projecting my frustrations on ducks.

"*Mademoiselle?*" the voice calls again, this time closer. "Welcome back. The usual?"

I shift in the chair to face the waiter. "*Merci*, Raymond, *oui*. Thank you, yes." He nods, and as soon as he looks away, I roll my eyes. Not at him. At myself. *Every time, you do that*, I think, chastising myself. *The simplest words in French, and you feel the need to say them in English, too.*

As if knowing this was a bad time, my phone buzzes silently from the pocket of my jacket. I don't even look at it, instead just feeling for the right button to make it stop.

The sun fades behind clouds to my left, causing them to glow in pink and orange as they flow across the purple-grey mountains in the distance. Buildings lie below those mountains, the western section of a city that curls around me in a layout all too familiar now. I've been in Geneva for over a month, and though I still fumble to speak a couple of words in French, I feel like I know every inch of the town. And of course they speak French here. As if I didn't get enough of that in Paris.

The fading sun makes me think of the last time I got a charge. It was my first week in Geneva, but really, I've used next to nothing of it since then, so I'm still pretty much full. That's a good thing. I'm an electromagician on my own, no one to back me up. Who knows when I might need a little EM power?

To my right is the massive water fountain called Jet d'Eau, and thankfully what little breeze there is carries its mist away from where I'm sitting. During my weeks in Geneva, I've spent almost every sunset at Raymond's little lakeside bar. Pretty sure every night I wasn't here was one where the wind would have made me and my chair damp with spray from the jet. Maybe the tourists enjoy running through the clouds of falling water for their silly photos, but after my first couple of nights here, I have to admit the fountain largely lost its charm, if it ever had much charm to begin with.

Raymond returns, arranging a simple wood slat table beside my chair and lightly thumping a stout, wide glass on its surface. "Enjoy, *mademoiselle*."

I smile. "*Merci.* Thanks." *You did it again, you idiot.* I raise the glass to my lips quickly, mostly in an effort to hide the grumbling, sour look that appears suddenly on my face. Maybe Raymond sees it, maybe he doesn't. He doesn't let on, either way. From his point of view, I'm an easy customer, I come back almost nightly, and I give him a tip each time for very little work. Probably better to let the weirdo chick sip her gin and tonic, and ignore her strange expressions. Besides, tipping isn't essential in Switzerland — it's already expensive enough here — so that alone might forgive my cultural and linguistic screw-ups. There I go, buying my way out of problems again.

And the city... It's not even all that big, wrapped around the southern curve of the lake and divided about in half where the Rhône River flows out, heading to the southwest. I looked up some stats. Geneva is only about six square miles, with a population of about 200,000. Both of those numbers are just a tiny fraction when compared to my hometown of New York, and still, after a month of searching, I can't find the two people living here that I desperately need to find.

My parents.

I take a longer sip of my drink, and realize something clearly. Things can't go on like this for too much longer.

No, not the search for my parents. Who knows how long that might take? They're clearly avoiding me. I mean, fifteen seconds after I got to Paris, not one but *two* groups of electromagicians were aware I was in town and immediately started following me. I can't imagine I've been this close to my own mother and father for this long and they don't know about it.

But *this*...? This daily routine of sitting by the lake with a chilled drink? Yeah, that's going to have to end soon. I place the glass back on the wooden table and rub my hands together. It's late October, and by this time in the evening, with the sun already gone, the temperature is probably in the low fifties. Generally, I like cooler weather, but I'm not some kind of ice queen. As a reminder, I'm an *electricity* queen. And no, that does not have a good ring to it, so let's forget I ever said that. Anyway, if it snows or the air temperature starts to feel about as cold as the ice in my glass, I'm going to need a new bar. Sorry, Raymond. It's isn't you, it's me.

I feel my phone buzz in my pocket again, and curiosity gets the better of me. Or maybe it's hope. There have been other EMs in Geneva; I've met a few. Either we're drawn to each other, or they know where to look for me. I may be an idiot, but I'm not a fool, if that even makes sense. Anyway, I think the EMs I've bumped into here at the least must know about my parents. Which is why I give every electromagician I meet my phone number. Something about the phone buzzing twice, back to back like that, makes me look at it.

It's my brother, Kevin. I flick it off again.

By the time I finish my gin and tonic, leaving cash under the glass for Raymond like I've done every other night, I feel cold to my bones. Sitting outside in the night air, beside a cool body of water, with the wind slipping over me and an icy rocks glass in one hand, I guess the warmth just gets sucked away. I start to walk, to get the blood flowing again, giving Raymond a quick wave goodbye.

Maybe tonight I find them. Maybe that's the last wave I have for old Raymond. I've thought the same thing for weeks now. I don't believe it. Frankly, I feel... I don't know, *lost*, even though I know exactly where I am. I don't have any of my normal comforts and fallbacks: Kevin, Juliet, Zee, and... Percival. No family. No friends. Just me. I've always tried to be self-reliant, thinking I could do everything all by myself. That might be why I can push people away so easily. Maybe I've been wrong.

Or maybe it's the cool Geneva air getting to me.

I shake my head and turn into the city, letting the buildings cut off some of the breeze. It isn't blowing strong, but now that I'm out of it, I realize how much it was sapping my energy. I reach into my well of electromagic power and stir up some juice. Not much — not even enough to make my skin glow bluish-white. Just enough to spark a flare of warmth in my belly. Weird how no one ever told me to do this when I'm cold. It's definitely been a welcome use of my abilities on these ever-cooler, always-boring nights. (For the record, I mean no offense, Geneva. But I didn't come here to sightsee.)

I pull out my phone with one bare hand, still warming myself from within using my power. I've practiced a lot recently. Funny how, once you get the hang of it, you can push and pull at the same time — flare a bit of power over here, tamp it down over there. I swipe to the recent callers list and tap my brother's photo.

A moment later, the phone call is connected, but for a second, no one speaks. "L— Lyn? Is that you?"

"Did you think someone else would call from my number?" I ask.

"No, it's not that." Kevin sounds genuinely surprised. "I just never thought *you'd* be the one to call *me*."

"Well, you have been blowing up my phone, especially this evening."

"I called twice."

"Within five minutes. Why?"

"Because I wanted to ask you to come home. Come back to the New York. Please."

I almost disconnect the call without another word, but that would just have him start calling me back, thinking there was some sort of interruption in the call, not understanding that I hung up on him. I hate that. Instead, I state the obvious. "Kev, I've already told you. There is absolutely nothing that will change my mind. I'm not coming back." There's a long pause, and I figure that's that. Maybe he'll finally get it and leave me alone.

Then my brother says something I don't expect. "The elders are all here in the city now, Lyn. They're ready. Torden Detonde has already been found guilty of murder and breaking his oath to the High Order. In a week, we carry out his punishment, which is, by rule, a public ceremony. We're going to use the Touchstone of Mount Hachiro and take away his electromagic powers forever, and I figured that of all people, you should be here for it."

My feet keep walking, back toward the flat where I've lived for a month in this odd Swiss city, but my mind has already left. Sure, I'm homesick for New York, though that can wait. But could I miss this opportunity, to see Torden get what he deserves?

I stop on the sidewalk, oblivious to a couple following behind who have to dodge my suddenly unmoving body. *Opportunity. It* is *an opportunity.* "I'll be home in two days," I say abruptly, then poke the button to end the call. Kevin begins some relieved reply, but I don't hear much more than his tone. Before he can pointlessly call back, I swipe through my other contacts, find the name I'm looking for, and tap to call.

"*Oui?*" It's my only greeting, but that's okay. I'm in a hurry, too.

There's no need to bother announcing myself. "I need to borrow something, just temporarily," I say.

"Of course. When?"

"Tomorrow," I say, cutting the line again.

Standing on a random street corner in Geneva, I start to plan my next steps carefully. My flat, straight ahead up the street, will be fine, I think. But I turn left, beginning to walk with the kind of purposeful stride I'd been missing for weeks now, given how pointless the search for my parents had become.

No more, I think, realizing with a warm certainty where I needed to go. *See you soon, Torden.*

2

A DIFFERENT ROUTINE

There's a knock at the door, not exactly light, but not a rude sort of banging, either. In other words, just enough to actually wake me up. Juliet, whom I consider a lifelong friend even if my brother pays her to cook and clean for us, is outside. "Lyn. Lunch is ready downstairs," she says with just the right mixture of gentle invitation and parental cattle prod.

When our car service driver Harry dropped me off yesterday afternoon, the first thing Juliet said was that she was glad to see me — happy that I was "safe and sound," as she likes to say. But her next words? Well, she was relatively kind about it, but they amounted to something along the lines of "you look awful, now go to bed." She must have seen the truth, because if I'm waking at lunch time, that means I've been asleep for something like sixteen hours. What can I say? We all have our skills, and sleeping is one of mine.

I throw on a hoodie and black jeans, because old habits die hard. Would I have been seen dead like this in Paris or Geneva? Not likely. Everyone there seems so stylish, so put together. A hoodie is either an announcement that you are a lazy American — I mean no offense to the great country of my birth here, the word *lazy* is describing me —

or you are someone from elsewhere wishing to jump on that lazy American train.

That's all a lot of words to say that I get dressed and go downstairs. My singular thought is that I am glad Kevin will already be off to work; I don't think for a millisecond that we'll have company. We do.

"Mornin' sunshine," Zee says as she drizzles some sort of dressing on her salad. Percival, one seat over, smirks with glee. Neither of these are things I wanted to see at my breakfast — scratch that — *lunch* table.

I'm frozen in the door for well over ten seconds, which annoys the shit out of me. Finally, I realize that it would be socially acceptable for me to speak. No, truly it was a social requirement. Like I know these things. "Hi," I say, clearly expecting that such a long and wordy diatribe rectifies any other faux pas I may have committed. Juliet appears, placing a salad at my usual seat, directly across from my friends. "Thanks," I say to her more out of habit than any true appreciation, which gives me a moment's pause. How easily I take the luxuries given to me. In Geneva, I had no housemaid. I got my own damn salad. I consider apologizing to Juliet, keenly aware that she wouldn't even know what I'm apologizing for. That's when I notice she won't make eye contact with me. *Wait a minute. She didn't just call me to lunch knowing Pers and Zee were here, she set this up!* For the second time in under a minute, I stand frozen in disbelief, just watching Juliet leave the room.

"You gonna sit and eat, or what?" Percival says, picking at the plate of greens before him, probably wishing whatever course comes next would hurry up and arrive. "Your salad's gonna get cold."

I roll my eyes as I plop grumpily into the chair, then perform a slow and dramatic unfolding of my napkin before draping it across my lap. Finally, I pick up my fork, stab at a lettuce leaf, chew the thing to death, and swallow. Feeling I had deliberately wasted enough time, I speak, trying to sound as if everything was normal. Also, even though the three of us know all too well what Juliet must know based on what she's seen, there is still the tacit agreement that no one speaks about EMs in front of her. This now seems wholly stupid to me, but I go along, anyway, mostly to avoid causing Juliet any embarrassment. Given that she's in the kitchen, I go ahead and speak freely. "So, how are you two doing? Working on anything interesting with the High Order these days?" *The High Order.* Those three words come out tinged with disdain, and so there goes my attempt at ice breaking.

"Actually, yes," Zee says. "You've heard of Jonathan Hemsmeyer?" I shake my head, resulting in a slight but noticeable sigh from Mackenzie. "He's the newly elected mayor of New York. Part of his campaign platform was to clean up the city, and he didn't mean hosing the piss out of every alleyway — *that* would have at least been a useful thing to do. Instead, the supposedly honorable Mr. Hemsmeyer wants to get rid of the homeless population."

Percival chimes in. "And not by, you know, giving them places to live, either."

I wrinkle up my forehead between bites. "So my brother has you getting into politics now? I'm confused."

Zee chuckles. "Not by choice, and not publicly, of course. It's just that Mayor Hemsmeyer's new policies have been turning up some strange individuals around the power plant. You know, *junkies*, but not the kind of junkies regular people expect."

"Regulars found EM junkies?" I ask, wondering what my brother Kevin and his precious High Order think about the possibility that they'll be exposed by our version of drug addicts. "What happened to them?"

Pers slides his mostly full plate of salad away. "First time it happened, they just *relocated* the junkies. You won't be surprised to learn the junkies found their way back. The regulars must have assumed the power plant was where the junkies were getting their drugs, and they were right. Just not about the *kind* of drug. Anyway, the second time, they put some of the junkies in lockup."

I thump my fork on the table. "They *jailed* people just for being EM junkies?"

Percival shrugs. "I guess they thought they could help them —

you know, get 'em off drugs and cleaned up. The problem was, without any electricity at all, the EM junkies just up and died."

Died, I think. *Just because they couldn't get juiced up.* Would I do the same, if I went without a charge for too long? Or, like Torden was about to find out, if my power was stripped away for life? I shudder, not wanting to find out, while a tiny thought in the back of my mind considers that the High Order might know the answer. And might be sentencing Torden to death, even though they could pretend all they did was take his power. Did I care? Wouldn't I kill Torden if I had the chance? *Probably*.

Juliet reappears, accepting an empty plate from Zee and me, and kindly taking away Percival's barely eaten salad without a word. Then she's off to the kitchen to fetch whatever comes next. Pers eyes the doorway with anticipation. For his sake, I hope the next course isn't something green.

Between my thinking and Juliet's brief appearance, Percival's comment about EM junkies remains hanging in the air until Zee takes up the slack. "So we rounded up the rest."

I scoff. "Kevin had you arrest EM junkies? I can't say I'm not unhappy to be a part of that little adventure." I intend for my tone to be *lightly chiding*. It comes out somewhere closer to *intense mocking*.

Zee snaps back at me. "We're not *arresting* anyone, Lyn. We're finally trying to help them. And before you even get started, I know it's because the High Order doesn't want some regular to figure out what an EM junkie is actually addicted to. Nevertheless, we're taking them in now. Kevin bought another building on the same block as our first. There, we take care of them. We're even trying to figure out how to ween them off of manmade electricity, to see if it's possible to bring them back. That has to be a worthwhile thing to do, even to an impossible cynic like you."

Juliet arrives, carrying three plates, each trailing intoxicating smells on little wisps of steam. Two hold steak frites — Juliet is not unfamiliar with Percival's carnivorous appetite and my kindred tastes — while the third is a small pile of ravioli. If I know Juliet, which I'd better hope I do after this long, the ravioli are stuffed with mushrooms, to suit Zee's vegetarian diet. Juliet even carries the two steak plates in one hand and the ravioli in the other, like they would otherwise be tainted. But Zee apparently has had enough of my bullshit. She stands and tosses her napkin onto the table. Pers, meanwhile, is torn; stay or go? The look on his face is like a classic British street urchin being deprived of his first meal in ages.

"I'm out of here. Sorry to trouble you, Juliet," Zee says in frustration before turning a withering gaze on Pers. "You stay and eat if you like." Then she slowly looks my way, her eyes narrowing to slits. She chooses her words carefully. "Listen, Lyn, I get it. The people we work for did you wrong. Your brother did you wrong, though apparently not so wrong that you chose to move out or anything." Ouch. That hurt. "But at least we're doing something. We're trying to live our lives and to make sure people like us can live theirs. I would think you'd give Pers and me that much credit, but it seems like you want to live with your head up your ass. When you decide you no longer tolerate the darkness and the smell, give me a call." With that, Zee leaves, takes the stairs down, and a moment later slams the front door on her way out.

As exits go, it's pretty spectacular. I'll give her that. As for the rest, getting along with the High Order, blah blah blah. No thanks.

Juliet, momentarily frozen by the outburst, looks at me expectantly. I nod, and she sets the two steak plates before us, taking Zee's ravioli back to the kitchen as she leaves.

"I bet you think I need to apologize," I say in the middle of chewing a bite. The steak is salty and delicious, with the frites just complementing the perfection.

Pers sighs. "I've told you before. I'm willing to meet you wherever you are. I'm not going to tell you what to do. No pressure."

I get angry, and I don't even fully know why. "No pressure? That is pressure! You and Zee go back to working for the Kevin and the High Order like it's nothing. How am I supposed to do that? They lied to me for years." I throw up my hands, gesturing to the very walls around us. "All of this, my entire world, has been a lie."

Percival swallows a bite of food then sits silently for a moment. "At least you have a world." Slowly, deliberately, he gets up, dabs his face with his napkin, and walks out, leaving me alone in the dining room.

What the hell is going on here? I think. Then a flood of memories hits me. Percival's father died of cancer when he was 18 or so. His mother remarried, and though she may be living happily somewhere, she generally avoids him, saying he looks too much like his father and it makes her sad. Pers has been living alone for most of a decade.

And that's the moment when I realize that he's talking about me.

I'm Percival's life, or at least his life that could be. And I'm taking that away from him. I'm even taking it away from myself.

Suddenly full of sorrow, I think about rushing out to stop him, but I don't.

Because in life, there are things we *want* and there are things we *need*.

Though half of me says it's a mistake to go it alone, the other half — the stubborn half — eggs me on. Being alone has been a conscious choice for so long. I'm *good* at being alone.

Then the other side of me chirps up again. Has it been a lie? Have I *really* been alone all this time? What would happen — what dumb decisions would I make — if I really and truly was left to do everything all by myself?

My stubborn half tells the rest of me to shut up. No more debate. I have something I need to do.

3
_____

FAMOUS LAST WORDS

"No funny stuff," the stiff electromagician guard tells me, someone I don't know. I don't even think I've seen him before, though he's about my age. Maybe he was one of Torden's Clan of Assholes. That would explain why he isn't familiar. All at once, I'm struck by the fact that my brother has guards, wherever they came from. And a prison. And, if they thoroughly searched me, they'd be pretty shocked by what they found.

"Do I look like I'm laughing?" I retort. The guard stands menacingly for a moment longer, as if he could actually intimidate me. Then, he moves aside and lets me in. Well, he lets me go through the metal detector. Yes, they have a metal detector.

Still eyeing me like I'm going to knife someone — which isn't far off my mood, given the situation — the guard gestures for me to follow him. "This way." He takes me down a hallway to a windowless door, unlocking it then holding the knob dramatically. "Like I said, no funny stuff."

I push past him and open the door. "Your point has indelibly been made."

The guard tenses like he wants to grab me and throw me in a cell. Yeah, he's definitely from the Clan of Assholes. But I'm Kevin's sister, and I have a bit of a reputation. He holds off, which is good, given what I could do to him at the moment. I turn back and speak in a low, threatening voice. "If anyone eavesdrops on my conversation, that person will be the next one in a cell. The next one to experience the Touchstone." The guard tries to maintain his swagger, but I see his forehead crease just a bit. He grimaces like he's smelling garbage, but nods nonetheless, probably happy to be out of my eyesight.

The door closes behind me and I find myself in a sparse room, everything a bland tan color. There are no windows, and only the one door where I entered. In the middle of the space is a utilitarian table with chairs on opposite sides. Handcuffed to one sits Torden Detonde.

"Hello, Lyn," he says.

"Shut up," I reply before sliding out the other chair and sitting to face him. "For once, I'm talking and you're listening. Don't interrupt me. I have a lot to say." I wait for some acknowledgement, but the best I get is a simple blink. Which is good; I guess he's taking me seriously. "You're a murderer and deserve more than just to lose your power. The Touchstone of Mount Hachiro is too simple a punishment for you. Maybe a public hanging would be better." I squint at him, trying to gauge his reaction, but it seems like Torden is at some kind of peace, not really responding to my words. "You killed countless EMs, including my friend, Robin, and my friend, Hayden. Right in front of my eyes, both of them. You created Stickmen and used them to extend your own pathetic life, all while living among us like some kind of wise old wizard. Then you built machines to do the same work — to take power from *us* and give it to *you*. Everything you've ever done has been for yourself at the expense of every other electromagician. Why anyone follows you, I'll never know, but here we are. You are finally about to be stripped of your powers for what you've done. How long do you think you'll last after that? A few years? Or worse? For someone like you, power mad, maybe the loss will be too great to bear. I hear that EM junkies have been dying from a lack of electricity. Are you any better than them? Once the Touchstone takes away your power, how much longer do you have to live?

Maybe just days." I sit there, my eyes burning holes into him. He says nothing. "If you have any sort of response, now's your moment. There won't be another."

Torden blinks once more, and for a second I think that's all he's going to do. Then he opens his mouth, taking in a great breath as he wets his lips. "I won't try to claim innocence for my crimes. I know what I've done."

"Then that's it?" I ask. "That's the end? You're pathetic."

"Maybe so, but know this. I may be the one who has told you the *most* truth."

I bark a harsh laugh. "You're so full of shit. You've never told me anything but lies."

"Oh really, Lyn? Who told you of your extremely high Quotient? Your brother? No, it was me. Who helped you find your special ability? Me. But, more important than any of those other things, who told you that they were lying to you? Who told you the High Order and the Prime Order and even your own family were *lying* to you? Who?"

He waits, though we both know the answer. I swallow, trying to quell the rise of bile in my throat. *It's fine*, I think. *It just makes this easier.* "None of that even matters. None of that atones for your crimes. You will lose your power and you will die, and all of that will be simple justice."

"And yet, you still won't find what you are searching for," he says plainly.

"Oh? And what is that?"

"Your parents, of course," he says, fixing me with a firm and unwavering gaze.

For a moment, I'm frozen, like the game is up. Then I look away, puffing out a breath. "As if you know anything of them."

"Child, I know *everything* of them," he says, leaning forward. "I know you've been searching Geneva to find them, and that you have failed."

"Because they aren't there," I say.

"Incorrect," Torden says, relaxing to press into the back of his chair. "I know exactly where they can be found, and Geneva is the place."

"They aren't there," I repeat. "And I should know."

"Of course," he says. "You've spent weeks looking around the city. But that isn't how you're going to find them. You have to realize by now that they are actively avoiding you."

The comment lands like a left cross, stinging me almost physically. At the same time, however, it's liberating. I stand up, then walk around the table to where Torden sits. Suddenly, he's concerned, even fearful. He's just an EM, after all, and a depleted one at that. He may have a little bit of charge left, but I have no doubt they had him use up almost everything, considering that they left him in a cell alone. Even with a charge, there's nothing he can do to me — I would just suck up any electricity he could throw at me. That leaves regular old physical harm as the only other threat, and I'm in good shape in my twenties, while Torden is over two hundred years old. If this turns into a kickboxing match, the odds aren't in his favor. I grab for his right wrist and he flinches.

"What the hell are you doing?" he asks.

I lean down and stare into his eyes. "I'm breaking you out of here," I say. From my pocket, I pull out three things: a long zip tie, a small, smooth white stone, and a key for the handcuffs. Thankfully, handcuff keys are pretty much generic.

"What is that?" Torden says with alarm, looking at the stone.

"Something I borrowed from your friend, Orkan Zidane, in Paris. You remember. Head of that *other* group, the Prime Order." I unlock the handcuffs, then quickly pull him up and zip tie his hands behind his back.

"What is it for?" he asks, still deeply concerned.

Forcefully, I pull his face before mine. "Like I said, I'm breaking you out of here. But I can't have you going rogue." I hold up the little white stone. "Orkan calls this a Quell Node. He used one on me and Percival in Paris, so I can tell you the effects aren't permanent. But, while it's touching you, you won't be able to use your power."

"I have virtually no charge in my body right now, anyway," he says, trying to sound sad and pathetic.

"Well, then," I say, spinning him around and placing the Quell Node between his tightly tied wrists. "This won't hurt too much."

With that, I fill myself with EM power and thrust it at the cinderblock wall. Having never done such a thing before, I'm not sure it will work, but I'm pleased when dozens of blocks blow outward to show nothing but clouds and sky beyond. Then I grab Torden Detonde, my sworn enemy, and fly us both out of his prison cell.

Boy, my brother's gonna be pissed.

4
_____

COVER STORY

"My dear girl, I fear you've truly lost your mind," Torden says from the back seat as I climb behind the wheel of my rental car. "Where are you taking me, anyway?"

I pull down the hood of my sweatshirt and adjust the rearview mirror so I can look him in the eye. "I have a gag and duct tape in the trunk. Pretty sure you don't want me to use them."

He breaks eye contact and looks out the window. It's late afternoon and we're at Newark Airport. I figure this is the best place to get a car and head south, and thankfully the rental lot is pretty quiet. "On the contrary, go ahead," he says. "You already have my hands tied behind my back and this damned *Quell Node* taking away my power. If you gag me, maybe I'll lean on the window to make myself easier to see. I'll make quite the sight for any passing travelers, wherever we're headed."

He's right, unfortunately. Breaking Torden out of my brother's EM prison is only a crime in the eyes of the High Order, and I don't care if they're upset with me. Gagging him and driving him somewhere against his will, however, is kidnapping and will land me in a real, iron bar hotel style jail cell if I'm caught. I don't revel in the idea of having a long conversation with the old coot in the back seat, but it's probably best if I'm going to pull off the stunt I'm attempting. "Listen. We're driving to Miami, overnight tonight. We're only stopping for pee breaks and gas, and if you don't go when I say so, I'm not going to be too worried about you sitting in your own mess. Got it?"

Accustomed to people who show him more respect, Torden grimaces like he's swallowed something rotten. Which would be fine by me. "This sounds delightful."

"Agreed," I say.

If there's a silver lining, it's that Kevin won't see any charge for the rental, or for gas along the way. Most importantly, he won't see the two tickets I bought. Technically, I'm still spending my brother's money, he just won't know how. I put fifteen thousand dollars on a reloadable prepaid credit card, which I've already decided to call my burner card. It means I can buy an awful lot of shit before I have to let Kevin or anyone else know where I am. Overkill? Maybe, but my brother won't miss the money. Actually, now that I know my parents are alive, I guess my brother's financial accounts are still technically owned by them. Whatever. They have a lot of money.

My first charge on the burner card is to get a new phone — I left mine at home, of course. My second is for the bandana (to be used as a gag if it comes to that), duct tape, and snacks. Gotta have snacks. The third charge is for the car. After a moment to consider if I've forgotten anything, I twist the key and the engine starts. I usually rent SUVs when I'm charge hunting, because frankly you never know when you'll have to off-road in those scenarios. This trip is different — highways all the way from Newark to Miami, eighteen-and-a-half freaking hours. I'll be absolutely wrecked when we get there, but I can sleep for days afterward, no problem.

There was one more purchase I made before the trip, but it was strictly a cash transaction. It isn't the kind of thing anyone wants listed, not even on a burner card.

As I pull out of the parking lot, I take a sip of coffee — of course I got coffee when I bought the snacks, I'm going to be driving all night. The first few minutes of driving are smooth sailing, until I get on the interstate and it's at a standstill. "What the actual hell?"

"Ah, the unpredictable whims of traffic," Torden says, far too happy to see my misery. "What's in Miami, anyway?"

I pound the steering wheel. "A boat."

"Oh?" he says. "Are we going sailing? Or, with all your *family money*, have you decided to live on a yacht?"

Since the traffic isn't moving, I turn around and face him, basically so that he can see my full, displeased expression. "Think of it as being for your own good. If my brother locates us, he'll lock you up all over again, and in short order, he'll use the Touchstone to take away your power permanently — that Quell Node touching you now is nothing in comparison. So I figured that the best plan of action was to go off the grid for a little while."

"And what exactly does that mean?"

"I bought us a couple of tickets on a freight ship. Two weeks at sea with no connection to the rest of the world. I think that'll be enough time to frustrate my brother's search. Miami to Algeciras, Spain, then another rental car over to Geneva. There, you help me find my parents."

"That is truly an elaborate plan," Torden says.

I give him a cutesy head tilt, then turn back to face the road. Nothing's moving so I blow the horn, perhaps the least useful human gesture of all time. "Oh, come *on!*"

Torden slips down in his seat, as far as he can, trying to get comfortable. "I hope your ship isn't sailing soon." He chuckles at his own words. "Well, there's an apt metaphor."

Desperately trying to ignore him, I check my watch and try to do the math in my head. Still plenty of time, but any other surprise traffic jams might be a problem. Red and blue lights catch my eye from the side mirror as a cop car approaches on the shoulder. I know he's probably heading toward an accident or whatever else is causing the backup, but I glance furtively at the prisoner in my back seat as a tiny bead of sweat forms on my forehead. "This is going to be a fun night," I mutter.

———

IT'S WELL past one in the morning and I'm doing nearly ninety. I probably shouldn't be, given that a simple traffic ticket would result in my imprisonment for kidnapping, but hey. Life on the edge, am I right?

"I hope you're wide awake at this speed," Torden says from the darkness of the back seat. Only the occasional splashes of bright color from the highway's street lights confirm that he's even still in the car.

"Feel free to doze off," I say. "I've got this." It's the first time we've spoken in over two hours. I thought he had his eyes closed, asleep. Besides, I was kinda getting used to the silence. Maybe too much, actually. The truth is, I could probably use someone to talk to, especially as it gets later and the number of other cars on the road dwindles. The drive is nothing if not monotonous. Generally just flat lanes of grey pavement forming ribbons to the distant horizon. Not exactly the kind of thing to excite your senses and keep you on the edge of your seat. Plus, I have a growing nervous thought that Torden is going to jump me somehow, or fly out the door, or otherwise do something I don't want. At least if he talks, I'll know he's still there.

"Sleep, my dear, may be somewhat impossible for me. Sitting this way isn't exactly the most comfortable thing for an old man."

"Spare me your claims of frailty and innocence."

Torden sighs. "I never claimed either. But I am over two hundred years old, and your zip ties are digging into my flesh. The only thing I can say I like about our current arrangement is having you as my chauffeur. Since we seem to have nothing but time together, can I ask you a burning question?"

In the rearview, wisps of Torden's white hair glow in a halo silhouetted around his head, lit from behind by the headlights of a distant semi. Most of the other drivers out at this time are long-haul truckers. "What do you want?"

He chuckles again. "That's my question."

"What?"

"Yes."

I swear to you, I almost swerve off the road and into a concrete barrier. I just want to kill the infuriating man in the back seat, but instead I bark in frustration. "What are you talking about?"

"Let's say you get us to Miami without incident. Let's say we take your boat to Spain. Let's say you drive us to Geneva, and I help you find your parents. *What then*? What do you want? What is the point of all this madness?"

"You're one to talk about plans and madness."

"Fine," Torden says, quite calmly. "I accept your assessment of me, but at least my plans have an obvious purpose. I have been working to fulfill my destiny."

"Your destiny? Bullshit. You've been trying to hoard all the EM power in the world for yourself, to make yourself important and get rid of everyone else. You've already extended your life that way. It's not destiny. It's an ego that knows no bounds and the unnatural results of what you've done."

Torden leans forward and I catch his eyes, lit by the pulses of passing lights. His gaze is steady. Determined. "My destiny is bigger than me or you, your parents, your brother, or your friends. My destiny is bigger than the High Order and the Prime Order, combined. My destiny is the destiny of all of us, every electromagician on this planet."

I spit a response, mostly because he's freaking me out. "I thought you hated that term."

Torden shrugs. "I use it because it's easy. I don't have to explain what I mean by EEMS." Enhanced electrical manipulation and storage, or EEMS, is Torden's supposedly scientific method of classifying us all, from one at the lowest to ten at the top. He says both he and I are level ten. I personally couldn't care less about his opinion of my ability. I'm only using him for some specific knowledge, then he goes back in my brother's jail. "Have you read Machiavelli?" he asks, in just the muted but still pompous tone you'd expect such a question to be asked.

"TL; DR," I say with a laugh, hoping he has no idea what that means. *"The ends justify the means... Better to be feared than loved... Violence may be necessary to stability...* Am I on the right page?"

"Good, Lyn," he says, smiling. "I'm glad to see that your wealth has not eclipsed your desire for knowledge."

"I doubt I would take it that far," I say, trying to recall where I even heard of Machiavelli. Maybe one of those history dramas? Definitely not from scholarly research. I didn't have a job until I was in my mid-twenties, and even then it wasn't out of necessity. You can bet I binge-watched a few shows over the years.

"All right, then. Sun Tzu?" He waits, his face dark with only his eyes visible in the rearview, surrounded by the halo of glowing hair. He looks like a mad scientist. No, worse. He looks like a person possessed by the devil, or possibly a demon himself.

I think. I know Sun Tzu is *The Art of War*, but can't recall much else. So I wing it, based strictly on the idea of war, and what I assume a man like Torden would do in such a situation. "Attack the weak points." My voice isn't as confident, but I still try to play it off like I know what I'm talking about.

Torden's eyes are frozen in the rearview. Then finally, he smiles, the corners of those eyes creasing. "Yes. Nice. Of course, Sun Tzu — or the collection of writers who called themselves that name — wrote thirteen chapters. Attacking weakness is merely one of his points, but you are correct, nonetheless. So, why do I bring up these men and their books?" I open my mouth to form an answer, but Torden doesn't wait for a reply. *Ah, of course*, I think. *He's busy grandstanding.* "They represent known ideals on how to overcome an adversary, though of course they hold only a fraction of such knowledge."

All this talk of adversaries and attacks has me confused. "Who are you at war with, anyway?"

Torden leans forward, straining on his seat belt, his eyes bright orbs in the mirror. "*I* am not at war, child. *We* are at war. All of us."

I chuckle nervously. "I'm not at war."

"Yet you take prisoners, as one does in warfare."

Shit. Good point. "Okay, fine. But calling the fight between me and you a war is going a little far, don't you think?"

"I'm not talking about you and me at war with each other, I'm talking about you and me and every other electromagician at war with humanity! We have been conquered and cowed by regular humans. Don't you feel it?"

Do I? Maybe. Am I tired of living like a freak who's not even good enough for the circus sideshow, where regular people might at least come, spend a buck, and take a look? I'm worse than that, aren't I? I'm the freak you hide in the back room, hoping the guests will go away before I start banging. I start to say something, but my mind and tongue get tangled. "I..."

Still Torden blazes with energy — not EM energy, just the passion of his convictions. "Aren't you tired of hiding in shadows when you know we are *superior* to them? Can you give me any good reason why things aren't reversed? Why we aren't running things while regular humans tuck themselves out of our way?"

Is that what I want? I think. I don't know that ruling the world is really on my agenda, but then again, it's not like I even rule the world of EMs. Somebody else — my brother, maybe — can do all that pencil pushing. But there's something very attractive about just being able to exhale in a public space, full of all sorts of people, EMs and regulars, and know that they know what you are. Know that you aren't pretending to be something else, just to avoid notice.

Torden sits behind me waiting for a reply, but I don't know what to say. The last thing I expected to do on this drive was to start having a heart to heart with Torden Detonde, the murderous asshole, and *agree* with him.

An orange light pops on in front of me. *Perfect timing*, I think. "We need gas. Next exit we hit with a station, I'm pulling in. That'll also be your pee break, so be ready."

Torden slumps back in his chair, puffing out a frustrated sigh.

———

I MANAGE to avoid becoming a convert to the Church of Torden in the wee hours, and when the sun finally rises, it feels like a moral victory. Still, there are hours to go. Checking my watch, I see that we should have plenty of time, so I allow us a 30 minute stop for fast food breakfast. I don't take Torden inside, of course — no sense advertising my crime. I don't even take him through the drive-thru, since I have no idea if some cash register clerk at a Brekkie's in the middle of Florida is going to go full-on vigilante on me and call the cops if they see him with his hands bound. Instead, I park, lock the car with him inside, and stand in line for our food. Right about now, I really wish Pers or Zee was here to sit with Torden, but I chose this path alone and now I have to deal with it.

Returning to the car, I fumble at the lock remote with one hand, while balancing a tray of drinks atop the other hand carrying our bag of food. Then I see it. The open door. I drop the bag and it makes a squishy splat on the pavement.

"*Shit!*"

My head is on a swivel, trying to look every direction. *Did he fly away? No, not possible. No charge. Did he even get out of the zip tie with the Quell Node. I hope not.* But Torden is nowhere to be found.

The parking lot, like virtually every roadside fast-food joint, is loaded with cars, providing approximately a thousand places where he could hide.

What is this guy, some kind of acrobat? How the hell did he get out of the car? I know there's a button to unlock the doors in the front seat, but the image of Torden's old ass somehow wriggling over from the back and hitting that button, what? With his nose? That seems impossible. Still, the door is open, and Torden is gone.

"Shit," I say again. I scoop up the food bag and deposit it in the front seat along with the tray of drinks. That's easy enough to do, since the *door is already open dammit dammit dammit!*

Then I begin a furious search through the parking lot, which is hard when you're also trying to make it look like everything is totally cool, no need to call the cops on me! Thanks!

I hear a muffled commotion off to my left, and head that way, basically praying at this point. There are two open, plastic picnic tables there, but as I round a large white van, I see a woman with a pair of small girls at a third table. She's looking away to the right with a strange expression on her face, and her breakfast sandwich, a chewed corner exposed from its branded wax paper, is frozen halfway to her mouth.

I follow her gaze, and there, thankfully, is Torden, shuffling off as quickly as he can in his crumbled coat and weird old-man hat. He looks like a vagrant or a drunk, his hands still zip tied behind his back. Luckily, the sleeves of his bulky coat at least make it a little hard to tell.

"Shit," I say a third time, this time low, under my breath. I hadn't wanted to break out my cover story, but anyway, here goes. "Grandpa! Where are you going, Grandpa! You know you need your medicine!"

The woman at the table and her two girls all spin to look at me, their faces concerned still, but now starting to shift toward relief. *Yes, ladies, someone is coming to take the old creep away. You're saved! Just remember: no photos, no phone calls.*

Torden staggers, looking over his shoulder. I can see immediately that he, too, has donned a cover. "G— get away from me! Help! This woman is trying to abduct me!" he shouts, in a carefully acted voice to make himself sound old and frail. He even cowers and whimpers a bit.

Yeah, no, you bastard. You aren't going to get away that easily. I turn to the family at the picnic table. "I'm so sorry for this. He's not all there anymore, and he needs his pills. Once I feed him some breakfast and get him his meds, everything will be fine. I'm sorry we interrupted your breakfast." I rush forward and, though he tries to wriggle away, I catch Torden by the arm as he nearly reaches the northbound side of the highway. A couple dozen feet away, a tractor trailer flies by, and I almost wish Torden had been in the road at the time. Then I realize that would've scarred the two little girls for life, despite the pleasure it would have brought me. I shuffle Torden around to head the other direction. "Listen, asshole," I whisper through a gritted smile. "I'm happy to gag you when we reach the car, so if you want physical punishment, keep it up."

"Help!" he shouts once more.

I raise my voice. "Now, Grandpa, come on. It's me, Mary Ann. You *grand*daughter," I say. The made-up name comes to me from nowhere, and I almost label myself his great-great-granddaughter, but figure I'll try to make it a little more believable for the onlookers, despite Torden's actual age. "Let's get you some food, okay? We don't want you to hurt yourself out here." I dramatically look toward the highway and its passing cars, then back toward the picnic table, and the mother gives me a caring smile. There you go. Now I know I've won.

Torden must see it too, because suddenly he slumps. "It was worth a try," he mutters. Awkwardly, I guide him back to the car.

I can't say I'm very gentle as I shove him into the back seat, but I at least have to make it look that way in case anyone else is watching. He hits his head, knocking the hat sideways with a grunt.

"Oh, Grandpa, be *careful*," I say, too sweetly. "Let me get you your breakfast." I turn in a wide arc, smiling to anyone and no one, like a pageant queen making sure everyone takes in the view, then retrieve the food from the front before rounding the car to open the other back door.

Yep. I sit next to Torden in the back seat because *this*, friends, is something I didn't think out fully. I have to hand-feed him his breakfast sandwich a bite at a time. He eyes me not with thanks or even annoyance, but with the absolute joy of one seeing someone belittle themselves for his convenience, and probably the pleasure of knowing he almost ruined the whole trip. And maybe could have gotten me thrown in jail for good measure.

In between feeding him, I stuff big bites of my own sandwich into my mouth, chewing vigorously as if my chomping was a way to fight back. "Clever attempt. How did you unlock the door?"

He doesn't answer as he chews, but wrinkles up his face in a way that emphasizes his bulbous nose.

I knew it.

5

SLOW BOAT

Hours later, we're rolling down a flat, grey highway on a bright, sunny day, with palm trees passing like pillars holding up the clear, blue sky. Finally, the port appears. Fancy, white cruise ships are lined up, loading or unloading their thousands of vacationers. They're like oversized tour busses for seniors at sea. When we reach the seedier part of the port, we see the cargo ships and their bustle, massive cranes moving shipping crates back and forth. It takes me some time to locate the correct one, but eventually I do. We come to the freighter *Sebastian Diego* flying a flag striped with yellow, blue, and red, a curve of white stars in the middle blue row. The flag of Venezuela, of course. How do I know that? Years of geographic studies? A well-rounded understanding of world politics? An interest in international sports? No! It says VENEZUELA right underneath the ship's name.

From the back seat, Torden barks a short laugh for no reason I understand.

I park the car out of the way to one side and pull Torden out of his seat, adjusting his coat sleeves to ensure they cover the zip ties at his wrists. For good measure, I take a thin sweater and double it over his hands — it's mine, but I doubt anyone is going to look at it too closely

— as if the old coot has just decided to walk along carrying this behind him. I give him the once over. Does he look like a kidnapped old man? Hopefully not. I just need to get him on board. This is another moment when I wish I had Zee or Pers with me — a distraction at the ship would be quite welcome right now. I even wish Kevin were helping, maybe paying off the crew to look the other way. But I only have myself. How many years have I told myself I was completely self-reliant? Uh, that would be basically my whole life. Now, here, doing the craziest thing ever — and that's saying something — I'm seriously wondering what kind of mess I've gotten myself into.

I pull up the barcodes for our tickets on my burner phone, then head to the back of the car where I grab my duffle from the trunk. Rummaging through it, I find the one other thing I bought, the thing I paid cash for. It's a plain, white envelope, and I pull two things out of it: fake passports. I grab Torden by the arm and lead him toward the gangplank where we can board.

This is it. Game time.

Carefully, I lead Torden up the ramp to where a white-uniformed man waits. "Come on, Grandpa. Watch your step, okay?" There, still acting like I'm concerned Torden might topple off the side into the water, I show my phone's screen as I hand over the passports.

The uniformed man accepts our little booklets with a strange expression, checking them both. He looks at one carefully, then at me, then nods before handing it back. A quick glance, and I see it's my fake passport; he's still holding Torden's. "You may board, miss," he says in an unfamiliar accent. Perhaps he's Venezuelan. Then he pulls a scanning device from his belt, ready to take my ticket... but seemingly *only* mine.

"With my grandfather, of course," I say, like I'm trying to convince the man. He ignores me.

Instead, he holds Torden's fake passport out — to Torden. "Each passenger must present his or her own identification." He waits. We freeze. It's awkward.

"M— my grandfather is quite old and sick," I say, trying to make us both seem pathetic. "Can't you just, you know, see that it's him? He's right here." I smile with the lower half of my face, but I'm pretty sure my eyes are trying to burn holes in this wannabe TSA general with his damned white uniform. *We're boarding a freight ship, for God's sake.*

White Uniformed Man is having none of it. "Miss, I'm afraid it's the law." He turns to Torden, still pushing the passport forward. "Sir?"

Torden being Torden, he thinks about it for a second, then tries to turn and grab the passport with a zip-tied hand. You know, pretty much making it obvious that his hands *are* zip tied.

With an incredulous expression, the man gestures toward Torden. "What's going on here? You cannot take this man on board this way."

I close my eyes and sigh. This is not going how I had hoped. How I had planned. *Maybe because you suck at planning*, I think. My mind reels. "Um. Yes. I'm sorry for this, but see, my grandfather is quite old, and his doctors fear he could sometimes be a danger to himself. That's why, well, you know." I smirk and tilt my head, gesturing toward Torden's clearly bound hands. Like everything is perfectly normal.

White Uniformed Man stomps his foot. Yes, he actually stomps his foot. "This is not possible. You cannot take a *prisoner* aboard this ship!"

Oh my God. Since when are freight ship workers so damned picky? *Okay. How would Kevin handle this? He would... um... escalate, I think. Take it to the manager.* "Fine, can you just call your captain, then? I'd like to work this out so we can get into our room."

That's when White Uniformed Man thrusts a finger at the stripes on his shoulder, as if I know what those mean. "*Señorita*," he says with a huff. "I *am* the captain."

Well, shit.

6

IN SECURITY

"A re you planning to drive?" Torden asks from the back seat, his tone annoyed but resigned. In the driver's seat, I'm scanning my phone, tapping buttons between bouts of idly biting one fingernail. I don't answer. Finally, he sighs. "Can you at least start the air conditioning or crack a window? This is South Florida, after all. It's hot out and getting even hotter in here." Still, I ignore him.

That is, I ignore Torden until I see motion in my peripheral vision, someone coming toward us. Check that. *Multiple* someones: the white-uniformed captain, flanked by two others. *Uh oh*, I think. Can't be a good sign that they came looking for us, especially when we just got bounced because Torden looks like my prisoner. Which, you know, he is.

With choppy movements, I turn the key to start the engine, and the AC pops on. The vents whoosh with hot air, blowing in my face, and I slap the plastic grill aside, recoiling like I've been punched. I hate having vents blow on me like that.

"Thank you," Torden says dramatically, as if I actually turned on the AC for him. The men are getting closer, so it's definitely time to get moving. I slip the car into drive and head for the parking lot exit as quickly but as calmly as I can. In the rearview, I see them stop. The captain raises a phone to his ear, and I imagine maybe he's giving someone my license plate. *That's not good. Not good at all.*

I know what my next best option is, but I don't want to do it. I just have a terrible feeling, all the way around. Still, I can't avoid it, so I head back toward the highway, following the directions I had just finished setting up on my phone.

Torden tries to talk, but this drive is in silence. Finally, I pull the car into a massive parking lot where noisy jets screech by overhead, and I find a spot that seems about as out of the way as possible. With the car still running, I get out, yank some vegetation from the overgrown median, and decorate my exposed license plate as best I can to obscure the number while trying to make it look natural and subtle. Side note: Thanks, New Jersey, for requiring a front *and* back license plate. It would have been so much easier to hide just one. I inspect my work, knowing it won't do a lot of good, but satisfied that if it gives us a few hours, it'll be enough.

I get back in the driver's seat and spin around, putting on my hardest expression. "Listen. Obviously, there has to be a change of plans. We're taking a flight to Europe. Kevin probably has guessed that Geneva or Paris is my goal, so we avoid those two. We're flying to Milan, Italy, and from there it's another rental car. The good news for you is that our little European road trip will be *much* shorter, given how much closer Milan is to Geneva than our original port destination." Torden tries to keep a straight face, but I see the corner of his mouth twitching. *You love that you screwed up my plans, don't you?* I think. "Something funny?"

He nods downward, indicating his bound wrists. "How exactly do you expect to get me on a plane *like this* when getting me on a freight ship didn't work?" He has a point. Security at the port was one uptight guy. Security at the airport will be metal detectors and x-ray machines.

I close my eyes and take a couple of breaths. Finally, I tilt my head up and lock his eyes with mine. "When we get inside the airport, I'm going to free your hands. And I'll remove the Quell Node."

Torden's bushy eyebrows raise with legitimate surprise. "You're letting me go?"

I bark a short laugh. "Hardly. You're still my prisoner, and you're coming with me, all the way to Geneva, until the job is done and you find my parents. If you try to escape from me, I won't just bring my brother and the High Order down on you, I'll call in the Prime Order and their militia. Besides, you're almost completely drained of power, and you're old, even by old standards. Hell, I'll call some of my friends, and we'll capture you. You won't even have a moment to charge up, so it won't be a fair fight. And if I need to, I'll physically harm you to keep you in line, understand?" He nods, but the slight grin remains. The old bastard is up to something, I know it. I seriously doubt I've seen the last of his escape attempts.

I've got a really bad feeling about this.

———

"I HAVE A DEMAND," Torden says in the wide entryway to Miami International Airport.

Back in the car, with gloves on to avoid knocking out my own power, I had carefully taken the Quell Node off of him and tucked it into a small bag, tossing that into my duffle. Then I clipped off the zip ties on his wrists. He was silent then, silent until now. Suddenly, with people flowing all around us, he speaks? This does nothing to calm my nerves, especially after his attempt to escape, which I will forever call The Brekkie's Incident. "What? And don't pull anything stupid."

Torden tilts up his chin, displaying a cheery grin. "I would like a book to read on the plane. And there's a little newsstand right there. I want you to buy me a book."

I eye him suspiciously for a long moment. "That's it? A book?"

"That's my demand," he says, giving a pseudo-serious nod to emphasize his point.

Shaking my head, I lead him toward the shop. "Whatever. Pick one quickly."

"Oh, no, dear Lyn," he says, feigning horror. "One does not enter a bookstore and choose quickly. One must take one's time, search all over, and make only the best selection for that moment in time. Or buy them all. That works, too."

I pull up to stand in front of him, my expression blank and cold. "One book, five minutes. You don't pick, I grab the closest romance novel I can find with the sexiest bare-chested man on it, and you deal with that."

He smiles. "What if I happen to like romance novels?" he asks.

I shudder, having no desire to imagine Torden Detonde feeling romantic.

———

TRYING to look innocent and unassuming in an airport security line when you're traveling overseas with only a basic duffle bag, while the old man next to you carries nothing but a single paperback book? It's not an easy task. Trust me.

Torden goes first, dropping his thick book on the conveyor. It's a science fiction book, thank God. I flat out disallowed romance options, knowing I'd have to sit next to the old creep. He's about to proceed through the metal detector when an agent gestures sharply. "Jacket and shoes, too, sir. And the hat," the man says. *Phew. Those are no big deal.*

Then it's my turn. I place the duffle on the rollers and slide it forward as I consider everything else I'm wearing. I slip out of my shoes, still keeping one eye on Torden as he walks forward. The machine doesn't beep. Good. One step at a time. Barefoot, I follow him through, and the machine remains silent.

On the other side, Torden retrieves his things and starts to put everything back on, as I stand in line waiting for my shoes to arrive, wondering how many barefoot souls have stood in this very place. Them and their questionably cleaned feet. No, best not to think of that.

"Whose is this?" a dark-haired security agent brusquely asks, holding my duffle in one hand. His hand is protected by a blue latex glove, making it seem like I have a bag full of anthrax or explosives.

"Me," I say, sheepishly raising a hand. *What now?*

"Follow me, ma'am," he says, guiding me to a bare metal table a short distance away. Behind me, other passengers continue to stream through security, on their happy way to who-knows-where.

The agent places the duffle on the metal table in a way that reinforces the feeling that he thinks it's dangerous. I start to sweat. No, I've been sweating. I sweat some more. "Unzip the bag please, ma'am." I do. He begins to rifle through it, using his gloved hands and a little prod-like stick. In another setting, he might be ready to conduct an orchestra with the thing, or toss it for his dog to retrieve.

"Is something wrong—?"

The agent finds a long, thin, plastic bag, fetching from the duffle and holding it up between us. "Is this yours, ma'am?"

"Y— yes?" Oh God. He's holding the bag of zip ties.

"Are you aware that zip ties can be used as a restraining device?"

You don't say? I try to fake it. "Uh, yes, but I just use 'em for stuff that, uh, falls apart."

"Like?"

I'm completely winging it now, hoping the security agent doesn't notice. But his face is stern and his dark brown eyes are locked on me. *Talk, Lyn,* I tell myself. *Say something, anything. In fact, say everything.* "Anything, really. But mainly, duffle bags like this. I've traveled all over, and I like to have a duffle with me all the time. Anyway, stuff falls apart, am I right? I must have had a dozen of these things over the years, and you know what always breaks first? The handles! Yep, the most important part! Well, I guess to hold things, the bag itself is important. So I guess all the parts of a duffle bag are important, but you can't carry it without handles, ya know?" I am intentionally droning on now, and I see the agent's face tense, his brown eyes narrowing. *Keep talking, Lyn.* "So, I learned the hard way to bring zip ties. Those things can hold anything together. When a handle breaks, just grab both ends, zip tie them up —"

The agent drops the bag back into my duffle dramatically.

"They're fine. Confiscation is at each agent's discretion. You can hold on to those."

"Oh!" I say with far too much manufactured joy. "Okay, thanks!" I start to zip up the bag to be on my way.

"Hold on," Agent Brown-Eyes says, a little too harsh. King of his domain, he is, and so I back down. He fumbles through the duffle again and pulls out my half-finished bottle of iced cappuccino. This time, he doesn't ask if it's mine, or try to get a story, he just holds it between his thumb and forefinger like it's contaminated. Without a word, he turns to the side and releases the bottle, letting it crash into a large plastic bin. The Airport Bin of Shame. I look down, puffing out my lower lip, and this time it isn't an act. That was caffeine he just murdered. Damn this brown-eyed man. "Thank you," he says, sliding the disheveled and unzipped bag toward me, and walking off without so much as an apology or telling me where my next caffeine might come from. Twisting up my face in irritation, I toss things back in the duffle and zip it up.

Then I freeze. *Torden!*

With security hassling me, I've totally lost track of the man. I quickly look around, just like when he disappeared at Brekkie's. Only, you know, now I'm surrounded by federal agents in an airport.

I don't see him anywhere. Torden is gone. I start to walk down the concourse, scanning every shop, every bar and restaurant. Gone. And this time, I fear, for good.

I reach an area where people are milling around on their phones, waiting for loved ones. The bathrooms. That's when it dawns on me that he could simply go in the men's room and wait. *Damn it!*

I consider barging in, but there's a constant stream of guys entering and exiting. Finally, I just ask one of the men coming out, an older black man in a nicely tailored business suit. "Excuse me, sir. Was there an old guy in there? Tan jacket, boots, hat over wispy white hair?"

The businessman looks at me strangely before shaking his head, his eyebrows raised over the weirdness of the question. "Not that I saw. But, I don't exactly take inventory in the airport bathroom." Fair point.

I stomp away, toward the gate, figuring I'll just toss my stupid duffle in a chair, then go back and wait at the men's room. He has to come out at some point, probably intentionally *after* our plane leaves, but at least I'll catch him.

Just before I toss the duffle into one of those ergonomically uncomfortable airport chairs, I see him. Torden is just sitting there at the gate, reading his book. He looks up. He even gives me a little wave, like, *over here!*

Realizing I have an utterly shocked look on my face, I quickly turn away, pretending to check something on my phone.

———

"Economy class, Lyn?" Torden says, disappointed.

"You could be on a freight ship for two weeks, instead." He grimaces and nods, accepting that rebuttal.

The doors to the plane are closed, and our flight attendants come by for a final check. I settle in, hood up for a semblance of privacy, seatbelt tight. I'm ready to be in a locked metal tube 30,000 feet in the sky, so I can stop worrying about Torden escaping for once. While EMs can hover in the air, I've never heard of one at such an altitude, and certainly never heard of one jumping out of a commercial plane. Plus, Torden is as close to out of power as he can be. Jumping out would be suicide, and given the effort he's put into prolonging his life, that doesn't seem like his style. I close my eyes.

And there's a metal clack next to me, the feeling of motion. Popping open my eyes, I see Torden jumping up, pushing past me to the aisle. I react. Not smartly, not given who he is, but it's a split-second thing. I fill myself with electromagic power.

"Sir! Please take your seat!" a female flight attendant says, just over my left shoulder.

Then everything happens at once.

I start to stand but realize the seatbelt has me stuck. I grab onto

Torden's jacket, though he's more nimble than I'd give him credit for. Already he's standing in the aisle. The flight attendant bumps me then yelps, jumping back, and Torden throws open the overhead storage bin. In a flash, there's something in his hand. The damned book. I release my power, all at once, as quickly as I can, and pull down my hood.

"You —," the attendant beside me says, shaking visibly. "You shocked me."

As Torden pushes back to his seat, I put on a weak grin and turn my palms up in innocence, my *Who, me?* gesture, trying to tell this woman I have nothing to hide. *Damn it. Play it cool.* "Um, sorry?" I say. And the old electromagician lies come back, easy as can be. Lies every EM has told a regular at some point, where there was some screw-up. "I must have shuffled my feet on this, um, thin carpeting." I gesture toward the floor, trying to look pathetic and divert her attention. "You know, static electricity?"

The woman doesn't bite. She looks at me from under a furrowed brow. I have a feeling she knows exactly what a static electric shock feels like and knows that wasn't one. But what else could it be, from her point of view? She stares at me coolly, a look I am not unfamiliar with from flight attendants, but finally turns toward Torden. "Please buckle your seatbelt, sir."

"Yes, thank you," he says, complying, his stupid novel resting on one knee. It's a thick tome, called *Force of Will*. The cover shows some ardent space warrior wielding a glowing blue sword in the face of a massive army of robots or armor-clad people, I have no idea which. The image makes me roll my eyes.

As the flight attendant continues up the aisle, I mutter a curse and speak softly to him. "That better be one great freakin book. But why the hell did you put it in the overhead?"

In response, Torden mimics my *Who, me?* gesture from a moment ago. Grin, palms wide, facing up.

It's a while before I'm calm again. Because despite the circumstances, I have the gnawing feeling that Torden is at least as much in charge as I am.

7

IL PUZZO DI PAZZO

T wo options exist between Milan and Geneva. Well, two reasonable options. I am sure there are others, such as another miserable plane ride, or hitchhiking, or hot air ballooning, but I'm not completely insane. Have you ever been in a hot-air balloon? Death trap. A flammable wicker basket hanging underneath a giant flammable balloon, with only a large gas-fired *flame* keeping you in the air? Oh, and did I mention it's completely rudderless, guided by the fickle winds? And your "pilot" has been huffing gas fumes for going on the past decade? So the hot-air balloon option is *out*.

There is, of course, a train. This is Europe, after all, and I understand it's a lovely ride through the mountains, very scenic. But another attempt at mass commercial travel is nothing I can stomach at the moment. We opt for the rental car. "But that's commercial travel!" you say. Well, first, I don't recall making this a democracy, so pipe down, you. But second, it isn't *mass* commercial travel. It's easy to put Torden back in the zip ties with the Quell Node, force him to sit somewhere in sight but away from the rental agency office, and rent a car without a lot of people trying to ask dumb questions like, "Why is he tied up?" or "Are you aware that kidnapping across international borders is a crime punishable by up to three years in jail?" See how none of that is helpful?

So, another car, another almost four hours, and then, finally, Geneva. And no, I don't just put the rental car in neutral outside of town and let it roll down some Swiss mountain. I return it properly to the agency by the train station. And also no, Torden does not quietly ride along. He's once again talking about power and warfare and shit I don't want to agree with him about.

From there, we walk to my old flat, still paid for and waiting. We only have a duffle bag and a book to carry, and besides, Geneva is a very tightly packed, walkable town. On the way up the stairs to the flat, I realize my landlord might see Torden and me together, which would just be... weird. But if we'll both be living here for a while, that's something I'm going to have to get over.

My landlord is an elderly gentleman by the name of Signore Bernasconi — he's Italian, says he's from the eastern part of the country, near the border, and of course he prefers to speak in his native tongue. As if keeping track of French and German weren't enough in this city. In any event, he's been super cool as a landlord, mostly because I almost never see him, he doesn't hassle me to pay (then again, I always pay on time), and he doesn't check up on my comings and goings. But add a new person who happens to be a man, and who's visually around the same age as Signore Bernasconi? I hope it doesn't become an issue. Plus, I can't imagine adopting the Grandpa cover story for the long term. Doing it twice was hard enough, and I despise the idea of anyone truly believing I'm related to this creep. Torden will have to be an elderly friend. Or maybe acquaintance is better.

I almost have the door to the flat unlocked when I hear Bernasconi's familiar raspy and accented voice. "She has returned?" he says, friendly but curious.

I turn to face him, the door still locked and the key dangling from its key chain with the oversized wooden cutout of Switzerland, something that manages to say *I'm a tourist!* and *Don't steal this key, you thief!* at the same time. "Oh, hi, *Signore*. Yeah, I had to go back to the

States for a bit to see my brother, but I'm back now." Over the weeks of my previous stay, it had become habit just to refer to him as *Signore*, nothing else.

Signore's eyes flit between me and Torden, and his implication is clear: *Who's your friend?* I ignore it. "Well, we need to go unpack!" I say with an overly friendly wave, realizing immediately that our need to unpack a duffle and a lone book were clearly minimal.

"Hello, sir," Torden says out of the blue. "My name is Torden Detonde, a friend of Ms. Hopkins. She has graciously invited me to stay for a while with her here in your fine city. I do hope that is acceptable to you." Torden manages an awkward bow, and I want to kick him. I specifically told him not to talk to anyone. Anyone. Why? Because, although he has his jacket on and it isn't obvious on casual inspection, his wrists are once more bound together by zip ties, with the Quell Node tucked between. I did it behind him, perhaps stupidly thinking that he'd look like an old man strolling lazily through the city, hands clasped behind his back. But standing on the stairs in front of my door? Bowing? More and more, his posture looks unnatural.

My landlord nods politely. "Of course! Welcome. My name is Luigi Bernasconi, but most people around here just call me *Signore*. I suppose elder statesmen such as us have earned these sorts of titles, right?" He chuckles, still eyeing Torden carefully. "I hope you enjoy your stay in Geneva." He gives us a little wave and starts to head back toward his own flat, which is in the rear on the ground floor. "Oh, and let me know if you see Pazzo. My little crazy has been away for some time, probably carousing with the ladies."

"Uh, sure. Will do." I wave a second time, but even as he walks off, I catch Signore giving us — well, giving Torden — a suspicious look. Maybe I dream it, but I'd swear he looks at Torden's hands and wonders why the old man doesn't wave back. Quickly, I twist the key and the door pops open with a loud click. "Inside. Come on," I say to Torden, gesturing too enthusiastically.

Once more playing the old man card, Torden hobbles up the last couple of steps, slowly and deliberately before ducking into the flat.

He stops cold, gasping.

"What?" I ask. "What's wrong?"

Torden looks over his shoulder toward me, his face wrinkled as if in pain. "Can you open a window? Or maybe *all* the windows? It smells like something died in this place."

I lean past him and sniff. Why do we all do that? It's like none of us believe another's ability to smell. Immediately, I regret it. *Rotten food? Something I left out? No, it doesn't smell like that at all... It's more like ammonia and...* Just then, a black blur zips past my feet and down the stairs. Signore Bernasconi's ornery cat, Pazzo. Must have been accidentally locked in my flat for days while I was gone. I don't even know how he got in there, but I suspect he snuck in while I had my morning coffee on the tiny front balcony. I almost feel sorry for the poor cat until I see the mess. Pazzo didn't just poop and pee all over the place, he also knocked just about everything down. From the doorway, I see a broken glass and soil from an overturned potted plant.

"I've just decided I'm a dog person," I say, holding my nose to enter.

———

CATS ARE AMAZINGLY efficient at making a mess when they want. Yet the funny thing is — if I ignore the floor — the flat looks remarkably clean. That is, of course, because Pazzo knocked virtually everything off the shelves, tables, and counters onto the floor. There, he rummaged through some things, ignored others, and even left wonderful little cat turd sculptures amid a few. As I clean, Torden sits just outside the now-open window, preferring the fresh air he can get sitting on the balcony. It's cold and growing colder outside, but better that than the enclosed stench of the flat. Fall seems to have departed Geneva while I was gone, and the air smells crisp, like snow might come soon, maybe even tonight. Out of habit, I pause and scan the weather app on my phone, but on the way, I realize the date: the second of November. *Man, I've wasted a lot of time in this city*, I think.

Good thing he's with me now. Time to get this done, and tomorrow's the day.

"I'd appreciate if you could get these things off my wrists," Torden says offhand, not even looking my way. He still has his jacket on, mainly because with zip-tied hands, he has no way to take it off, and it is cold sitting on the balcony. The jacket also conveniently covers his bound wrists, for the most part, though whether I bind his hands in front or back, it still looks strange. I just have to hope no one notices such a minor oddity in an otherwise already odd-looking old man. Of course, I would prefer he doesn't talk about any of this out in the open, even if that's just my balcony.

"You're hilarious. Now be quiet," I say, still cleaning.

"This is no joke, child. Did you see the way your landlord looked at me? I can't move like this. People will notice."

He's, sadly, correct. I keep cleaning, trying to ignore him.

"You can't ignore it," he says, as if reading my mind.

I throw a wad of napkins in the trash, along with whatever disgusting thing I just mopped up with them. "Sure. I'm going to cut those ties and take the Node. Then, first chance you get, you're gone."

Torden turns to me, his wispy white hairs fluttering in the cold breeze. "Let me guess. You think you'll see your parents tomorrow."

I freeze, just for a moment. *Is he reading my mind? No, that's impossible.* "Maybe not tomorrow. But very, very soon."

He leans toward me, nose poking through the open window between us. "Lyn, you have no idea what we have to do to gain access. It isn't like I'm going to lead you to them in the morning. I don't even know where your parents actually are."

I slap a hand down on the thin counter that makes an L in one corner of the main room, the area that constitutes my kitchen. "Then what the hell did I bring you here for? Why bother even breaking you out? I guess I'll call my brother and tell him where he can find you."

Torden shakes his head quickly. "Now, now, don't get hasty. I don't know where your parents are, but I know how to get to them."

"And how do we do that?"

"Like I said, it isn't just one simple thing. It takes a series of steps to get to those two. They didn't want anyone just stumbling into them, then spreading rumors or, worse, outright telling others where to find them."

"You're full of shit," I say, scanning the room and seeing other areas still in need of cleaning. I head to the nearest one, dragging the trash can behind.

"You very much love dismissing my knowledge, so I will simply move past that comment. The fact is, I know where we can begin, and I am familiar with what to do after we begin. You know nothing, though you act as if you have all the answers. If you want me to help you, and I can't imagine you took me here simply for a Swiss vacation, then you need to cut me out of these ties so I can lead you to the right places in the city and get things underway. I tell you in full truth that I cannot help you find your parents while I'm tied up like this. We will need to be in public places, and this simply will not do."

Whether or not he's telling the truth, I know he's right about one thing: walking around the city with his hands bound is going to be impossible. At the very least, it means I have to hand-feed him, and I'm quite tired of that already. Given my current status neck-deep in manual labor, I relent. "Fine. I'll cut the ties. But the same rules apply as with the flight over here. You try to run, and I rain hell on you." One thing I'm glad about: the door is keyed from both sides, meaning that I can put the door key in my sweatpants pocket at night and Torden would have to jump me to get it. At which point, I would, of course, beat the crap out of him.

"I will do as you ask, Lyn," he says, rising and turning around so I can get to his hands.

I go back to cleaning. "Not now. You think I'm falling asleep in here tonight, with you free? No way. Not on Day One, that's for sure. Have a seat."

Voicing his displeasure, he does, plopping down as a strong, icy breeze kicks up. Torden pulls his chin down into his coat, like he's a turtle trying to hide in his shell. "Well, I do hope you'll be done soon so I can come in."

The first flakes of snow slither by on the flowing wind, and I smirk. *Eh, a few more minutes won't kill you, old man.* I pull up a little bit of EM power to keep me warm, wondering if even Torden knows to do such a thing. Seeing him shiver on the balcony, I don't think so, and that's just fine with me. *Better for me to be the one with more tricks up my sleeve*, I think, tossing broken glass into the trash and muttering a curse at Pazzo, that crazy cat.

8

THE CASTLE

Before I snip the zip ties holding Torden's wrists, I check the forecast carefully. I don't want some unexpected thunderstorm to pop in and provide him a convenient way to juice up while his hands are free. There's nothing. I realize I'm being paranoid, as the morning is cool, clear, and crisp; it's not exactly prime thunderstorm weather. The snowfall from last night is just a delicate dusting, only enough to be a bit of a nuisance in places like the stairs outside my flat, but it's so cold out today the flakes won't melt for a while despite the sunshine.

Rubbing at his free wrists, Torden looks at me with mild surprise. "That jacket, those shoes... My dear, Ms. Hopkins! You look positively... *fashionable*. I do believe Europe has changed you."

"Shut up," I say. I turn away before he can see my cheeks flush, wishing I had a hoodie to pull up.

A short while later, I make him come with me to get pastries for breakfast at a little cafe down the block. The owner, a young woman named Wilfriede, gives me a friendly wave. I wave back, but suspect she sees the scowl on my face. If she guesses it has to do with my unexpected companion, she's right. Torden and I head back to the flat to eat, each of us carrying our own little paper bag of food and a recyclable cup of coffee. My coffee is extra large this morning; I feel I'm gonna need it.

All I want is to get this done and return Torden to a prison cell, so he can suffer the fate he deserves. Still, I wonder which is worse: to let him live without power, or to kill him outright? Though I'd be happy to see him dead, I have to admit Kevin's plan to strip his power has its charm. Plus, given how unnaturally Torden Detonde has extended his life, maybe taking away his EM ability will suck away all that stolen life. Maybe they're the same thing. Either way, I'm anxious. Still clutching my half-finished coffee for warmth and the pulse of life it gives my body, I pull open the front door and turn back to Torden, who stands in the middle of the room finishing the last bite of his pastry. "Ready?" I ask.

"Are you?" he returns ominously.

I fix him with a blank stare. "I've been roaming this city for weeks and the best I have is a few errant EMs I bumped into by broadcasting my voice. We exchanged phone numbers, but they don't return my calls. So, yeah, I'm annoyed, tired of all this, and more than ready."

Torden chuckles, speaking to himself. "That sounds about right." He dusts crumbs off his fingertips, not concerned that they are dropping to the floor I just spent a lot of time cleaning.

"What? What is this series of steps you mention? What do we have to do now?"

"I asked if you're ready, because I know something about you, Lyn Hopkins. Young, impetuous, idealistic, yet demanding and prone to seemingly irrational leaps of... faith? Or perhaps merely leaps of understanding. In any event, what I know about you tells me something clearly. You aren't going to like this process."

"Why?" I ask. "What's the first step?"

"We're already doing it," he says, sitting back down on the couch.

"Come on," I say. "Stop fooling around."

He looks at me with a devilish gleam in his eyes, and I start to think this whole thing was a mistake. What was I thinking? Torden can't be trusted. He probably doesn't know anything, either. I just got myself in trouble with the High Order for nothing, and I'm shacked up with a madman who's very likely to try to kill me in my sleep. Suddenly, a voice booms in my head. Torden's voice.

This is Torden Detonde. I have come to Geneva because I would like to arrange an audience with the Officials.

Two sentences. Then he's silent.

"What the hell was that?" I ask.

"*That* is step one." He idly flicks a crumb off his pants leg, once more ignoring the fact that it ends up on my floor.

Though I can see the crumb, sitting like a tiny beacon of my discontent on the wood parquet, I push it out of my mind. "Okay, now what do we do?"

"Now, child, we wait."

———

"I HAVE QUESTIONS," I say after twenty minutes or so of boring silence.

"Ask away," Torden replies. "We do seem to have time." This amuses him, and I can imagine why. Every moment he delays, sitting around in Geneva, is a moment he isn't getting his power taken away.

"First, how do you know someone from the High Order didn't just hear your message? We went to a lot of trouble to get here unseen by those folks, given how they desperately want to recapture you, and very likely want to try out some sort of punishment on me, too. Then, what? You shout your name to the whole town?"

Torden nods slowly. "A reasonable point, I agree. But the process demands notification of arrival. Besides, Geneva is known to be sparsely populated with EMs, but those that are here are usually Prime Order. If there happened to be some overenthusiastic High Order soldier out there who wants to report us, I figure that still means your brother and the others have to get a phone call, make arrangements, and fly here. That will give us at least a little time."

"Not much," I say with a huff. "Fine. Second question: Who are *the Officials*?"

This time, Torden just laughs. "You amaze me, Lyn, with how

much you don't know. But I understand. Powerful forces worked hard to keep you in the dark. To keep you untainted and safe, as if such a thing were even possible. Your parents, delusional as it may be, thought that if you didn't know things, you wouldn't be a target. Yet here you are. In my mind, you are the prize. But you know this already. If I were free to do as I please, I would spend all my efforts to learn from you the things you can do."

"*Learn*, yeah right. Your version of learning from me is to rip my power away and turn me into a Stickman."

Torden grimaces, but turns up his palms to me. "We admire the work of a surgeon to save lives, yet does a surgeon not cut with a scalpel?"

"Don't change the subject. Who are the Officials?"

"Your parents, of course."

"What's with the name, then?"

"They have to be called something, and I suppose they thought King and Queen were too grandiose." He's clearly toying with me again. "But this tells me a lot, Lyn. You say you've been here for weeks with no progress. That makes sense now. You don't even know who to call."

As if fate itself is seconding Torden's sentiments, static pops in my head and I hear a voice.

Torden Detonde, acknowledged. Meet at Jardin Anglais, today, noon.

Understood, Torden replies.

I slam my hand on the side of the chair. "Damn it!"

Torden looks at me sideways. "Does progress bother you, child?"

"No, not that. Just the place. Jardin Anglais. That's on the lake, right next to the bar I've gone to just about *every night*. Are you really saying I was that close?"

As he looks at me, I can almost feel the swirl of thoughts behind his eyes. Respect for how strong I have shown to be, and yet disdain for how naïve. "No, Lyn. Without knowing the process, you were never close at all."

————

"WHATEVER HAPPENS, STAY OUT OF SIGHT," Torden says to me as we walk down the wide sidewalk of Avenue Pictet-de-Rochemont — and no, I have no idea how to pronounce that properly. What seems like an endless stream of scooters, motorcycles, and tiny cars goes by on our left, and the air smells like a combination of wet cement and car exhaust as the dusting of snow slowly melts. Another scooter zips by almost close enough to touch, making a *brrrap* sound so loud that I shake my head from the unexpected pain. It's amazing how such a tiny thing can be so damned noisy.

"You've said that twice now. What's the big deal?" I reply.

"Listen to me and follow the process. I announced myself. You have nothing to do with it — not yet, at least. Do you understand?"

"Yeah, yeah, don't get excited. But I'll be watching closely. If you do anything that looks like a double cross, expect pain."

"Don't trust me, eh, child?"

I don't answer. Do I need to? "What are you going to do, anyway?" I ask.

"I'm going to submit my petition."

Well, I think, *that clears that up.*

The road bends and in short order the park appears on our right with a sliver of blue lake just beyond. I check my phone. 11:57am. Plenty of time. "Where do you think they'll want to meet up? It isn't a huge park, but —" Static pops in my head, startling me. *Meet at the clock.* "Shit, that scared me. Are they watching us or something?"

Torden shoots me a frustrated look. "You better hope not. Where is there a clock in this park?"

Clock? Like a tower or something? I can't think of any. Oh wait. *That* clock. "The flower clock. Far side, near the road. It's large, you can't miss it."

"Fine," Torden says. "Then I take the side of the park near the road, you go over to the side near the lake, and we'll head toward the clock. When we get there, you *stay out of sight.*"

"I said I got it." My hackles are up now. Torden is so adamant that it can't be a good thing. Still, I split off and walk along the lakeside. As we go, the static voice in my heads repeats its message about meeting at the clock, every 30 seconds or so, which acts as both a helpful notice and a somewhat nerve-wracking timer. Torden and I mirror each other's pace for the most part, while trying not to look connected and tense. Okay, the tense part is me. Torden seems fine. Every once in a while, I pause to look across the lake. I can see Raymond's bar, just off to my right, with the tall spray of the Jet d'Eau nearby. *I can't believe I sat right there so many times, and now here we are meeting up with my parents' people.* I turn back to see Torden has gotten ahead of me, so I move.

The flower clock — *l'horloge fleurie*, in the local parlance, though like many things it's just a fancy way to say the exact same thing — is on a slanted mound of earth at the edge of the park. It's a functional clock and, for some unknown reason, a tourist draw. I can already see a couple dozen people edging for position near it, taking photographs. Of course, being a clock, I guess it's also the perfect way for the person we're meeting to know if we're on time.

I have no idea which of the supposed tourists around the clock is really our man (the voice in my head is distinctly male). Torden approaches, then stops directly in front of the clock as if to admire it. When I was a little kid, I remember someone gave me a clock kit as a birthday present one time. It consisted of a tiny motor to drive the hands, and a battery compartment. Drill a hole in almost anything, stick the motor in the back and some hands on the front, and *voila!* Instant clock. That's about how impressed I am by the flower clock. By the way, I'm pretty sure that clock kit I got was a regift. If I had been a smarter kid, I should have regifted it again.

Torden is still gazing at the slowly moving hands, like nothing's happening, taking up a prime spot right in the middle of the action. Some tourist bumps him, and they exchange apologies. Then he glances once quickly to the side. If he's looking at a person, that person is hidden behind the dirt mound, out of sight for me.

I stroll around the park's walkways, trying to get an angle while staying distant, but the person seems to be in the worse possible spot. On purpose, of course. Behind the mound, to the far side, obscured by dirt, flowers, and a row of hedges, as well as the ever-changing mass of tourists. I continue walking toward the road, keeping Torden in the corner of my eye, straining to find out who he's meeting and what's going on. I don't trust Torden, and I certainly don't trust an unknown, unseen, shadowy figure Torden wants to meet. I have to know who it is, make sure Torden isn't planning to escape or to stab me in the back. As I slide over further, I'm trying my best to look casual, though I can't help that my eyes are fixed on the space in front of the clock.

Who is it? The young guy taking photos with his phone? The businessman in the suit who looks like he just wants to cross the street and get away? The old man with the tour book of Switzerland tucked under one arm? Then I see a person glance at Torden. Grey hair, dark jacket, a very European-looking leather bag hanging from one shoulder. I don't know him, but I feel sure. *It's him. Gotta be.*

Just then Euro-bag-man turns and looks me directly in the eye. I freeze. Torden quickly looks my way, then back at the clock, trying to pretend I'm not there. It doesn't work. Euro-bag-man huffs, turns, and walks away, quickly blending into a large group of tourists crossing the main street.

For a brief moment, Torden hangs his head, then he comes over to me. My eyes flit around, looking at anything except him. Like looking at him will admit what I've done.

"I told you to stay out of sight," Torden says, his voice coming out in a growl. "Did you really think you wouldn't be recognized? Anyone who works with your parents will certainly know you on sight."

"You've tried to kill me on more than one occasion. I'm supposed to trust you?" I stand straight, trying to look as if I'm in the right, even though I feel like an idiot.

"Yes!" Torden says gruffly, nearly shouting. "In this case, yes! Do you have any idea what you've just done?"

I wave my arms dismissively. "I messed up your meeting, okay. Sorry. Just, you know, call them again, and set up another meeting."

"It isn't that simple. Not that simple at all."

"Why not?"

Torden looks at me like I'm the dumbest person he's ever met in his life. "Because now your parents know that you're with me, and you are the specific person they're hiding from. I tell you to stay hidden and you walk right out where you can be seen."

"I said sorry."

"You say that, but I doubt it's true. This is just who you are, Lyn Hopkins. Independent to the point of being brash. You don't listen. You always do what you want. And that is why you *still* are not allowed to see your parents."

9
————

GODS PLAYING POKER

"Imagine," Torden says, chewing. "Just imagine what it would be like to live in a totally new and different world."

I lower my fork and fix him with a flat stare. "I'm an American living in Europe for the past month. I know what it's like to live in a totally new and different world."

Torden laughs. "This? This is different? Perhaps the language, a few customs, but really? When it comes right down to it, you've lived in New York City for your whole life. You aren't some Midwesterner, used to wide open spaces and even wider-open supermarkets and megastores. You can get along just fine in Geneva. I'm talking about true, systemic change."

I poke at my *salade gourmande de chèvre chaud* — salad with goat cheese — as Torden enthusiastically slices his *côtes d'agneau* — lamb chops. They say everything sounds fancier in French, and damn it, *they* are right. The entire little table shudders with Torden's violent back-and-forth rhythm, like he's a mad lumberjack carving up a sequoia rather than just some old dude with a dull kitchen knife found in the drawer of a rental flat, trying to get his red meat fix. Not many of the nicer local restaurants like to do carryout, but in the weeks I've been in town, I found a few. *Valanne Chalet* is, by far, the best, and as such it takes, by far, the longest wait to get your food. So dinner comes late tonight, we're hungry, and despite the quality of the food, we're pretty much inhaling it. I picked up a bottle of red wine while we were waiting on food, so I twist the cap — no fancy cork for us at *Chez Hopkins* tonight — and pour myself a glass.

Torden looks at the glass, then at me, his pupils partially hidden by the tufts of his long, white eyebrows.

I keep eating, pretending not to notice.

He does it again.

"Is there something you want?" I say between bites.

He clears his throat, going back to cutting his lamb, but far less enthusiastically. "Nothing. I was just wondering if you planned to drink all that wine by yourself, or if..."

I snatch up the twist cap and hold it between us. "Whatever I don't drink, I can just save for tomorrow."

His face twists and he concentrates on his cutting once more. "Yes, of course."

Still holding the cap, I watch him work, seeing how hard he's trying not to look at me. "Would you like some?"

"Oh," he says. "Oh, well. Only if it's not a bother." I stand, turn, and walk toward the sink. In the small drying rack there is another glass. Not a wine glass. This isn't a three-star restaurant. The glass is just some sort of tumbler. I grab it, hearing Torden shift in his seat behind me, no doubt in anticipation. Then I head back to the table, and pour him some of the wine, thumping the stout little glass on the table beside his dish. "Why, thank you!" He sniffs at the wine like I'm the sommelier at the fanciest restaurant in town, and foolishly I act the part, waiting for his opinion. "Smells lovely. Then again," he says, "I have been incarcerated for a while, so, you know... any port in a storm." He takes a swig, swirling it around in his mouth to get the most out of the flavor. Then he leans back in his seat, tilting his head up, eyes closed. You would think I just served him a thousand-dollar bottle, not the first red I could find at the nearby market.

"There you go," I say. "Now you're living in a totally new and different world. The world of cheap French wine." I raise my own glass, give him a little salute as he opens his eyes, and down half of my drink in a single gulp.

Torden smiles at me, then raises his own glass. "In New York, I bet a restaurant would charge a lot for this wine. Here, you bought it next to the cash register at a small grocery."

"Another new and different world," I say.

"Yes!" Torden lights up. "I was asking you about what you would think, but not about European culture, or wine, or any of this. About our entire world, a planet ruled by regular humans. And why? Because they are the most advanced, most powerful species on Earth. Or were. Until we arrived."

"Please spare me. I'm trying to enjoy my dinner." Even though I'm already eating, my stomach growls just a little, as if to back me up.

"Don't worry, Lyn. I'm not preaching to you. How could I? I'm just a prisoner. I just want you to *imagine* it for a moment. What would you do if you could walk outside right now, and regular people *knew* you, respected you? Understood you were someone of power? If nothing else, isn't this something we — *you* — deserve? I mean, take away any thoughts of world domination. That's not even what I mean. What about equality? Are you equal now?"

"Absolutely," I pop back.

"Really?" Torden sips his wine again, and I do the same. My glass is nearly empty, so I fill it again. "If you're equal, tell me this: what happens to you if someone catches you one day? Maybe you're gathering a charge via a lightning strike — you could pretend to be hurt and they'd probably let it go, probably even tell you how lucky you are to be alive." I look away left, not wanting him to read in my eyes the basis in truth such a scenario has. "That's one thing. But what if they see you doing something else? What if someone sees you shooting a bolt of electricity from your fingertips, or filling yourself with power and floating into the sky? If a regular sees you doing any of those things, what do you think they'll do?"

I answer before my brain can tell my mouth to shut the hell up. "They'd gather their torches and pitchforks, and then chase me into a barn and burn it down." My gut twists angrily.

Torden wrinkles his forehead. "A little melodramatic, but fairly accurate. Regular people will turn on you. Whether they shun you or try to lock you in a cage, they will not treat you as their equal. But what if they did? What if we came forward — all of us, many thousands — and not only announced ourselves to the world, but *demanded* our rightful place, as the equal to every other regular?"

"Even then, we aren't equals. If they knew what we could do, how could they possibly treat us the same as any other regular without EM power?"

"Exactly, Lyn. Exactly!" Torden leans forward, his body tense with excitement. He finishes his wine with a great wave of his hands. Meanwhile, my stomach lurches, and I think that'll be enough wine for me. I don't even say anything when he pours himself a second glass. "When we are known by the world, they will have to do the next logical thing."

"And what is that?" I ask. A burp rises suddenly in my throat, and I quickly cover my mouth with the back of my hand. I stifle it, but deep inside me, something rumbles. I realize that I feel rather warm.

"They will have to *respect* us, Lyn. We deserve it. You deserve it. We are strong, and we can do more than any regular. For that, we deserve their respect."

His excitement for the idea translates into an intense gaze, and suddenly I want nothing more than for that gaze to focus on something other than me. "You mean fear. You want them to fear you. That's not the same thing as respect." A loud growl comes from my abdomen, and I see Torden recoil slightly, dabbing his napkin at his chin.

"Are you all right, child?" he asks.

"Fine," I say, curtly.

"All right. So this world I describe. Can you imagine it?"

"No," I say, once more blocking an unexpected burp. "No matter how, if we appear and show people what we can do, they will turn. They outnumber us by a ridiculous amount. All I can imagine is EMs as lab rats and circus freaks." Pain hits me in the gut and I tense up. I realize I haven't even touched my salad in some time, so I reach for my fork. As if my body is against the idea, the pain in my stomach doubles and I wince, letting out a sharp breath.

"Child, child... No faith. No belief in your own people. No imagination," Torden says, sipping wine again. "You probably don't even believe in a place where lightning rains down from the sky every day."

I laugh, though it's cut short by another burst of pain. "Wouldn't that be nice?" My stomach twists again, hard, and I have that sensation that says *Get to the bathroom right this very second or else you'll regret it!* I stand and quickly stumble toward the flat's single tiny bath.

"And yet it's true," Torden says as I shove the bathroom door closed behind me with a loud thump.

Just before I vomit for the first time, I hear him sawing at his lamb again. He's even whistling a joyful little tune.

10

LIGHTNING FROM A CLOUDLESS SKY

I think everything I've ever eaten has come up. It can't just be from today, or even this week. I got rid of everything.

I'm sitting on the tile floor of the bathroom, leaning over with my head against the toilet. In some deep recess of my brain, I curse European commodes like this one because it isn't made of hard, cool porcelain. Mine is plastic, and it just isn't as comforting when your head and stomach have packed bags, bought tickets, and jumped a train to get the hell out of your body. And did I mention the sweats? Yeah, I shouldn't mention it. Don't start to picture me like this. It's ugly.

I'm not sure if I've been awake the whole time, but I think the answer to that question is no. It feels like it's been a while, and it dark and quiet outside the bathroom door.

Dark? Fine. It got late.

Quiet?

Oh no.

He's just asleep, I tell myself. *Don't freak out.*

I freak out.

I start patting my pockets, hoping but not expecting. My head throbs and my stomach gurgles a new protest, forcing me to slow my efforts. I have four pockets, but I methodically check each one three times. It doesn't matter; I know what I've done. "I left the front door key out there with him," I mutter, barely audible. "Shit."

I try to stand, but my entire body screams *No*. Worse, my headache seems to be directly proportional to its distance from the floor. Even raising my head a few inches feels like spikes are being driven through my temples. But I can't just sit here, knowing that Torden may be trying to escape. I slide sideways, to the cabinet under the sink, opening the door to see if some blessed soul might have left some aspirin or other pain reliever in there. Inside I find a random assortment of strange things: a couple extra bars of soap, an old pair of rubber gloves, a bottle of some sort of all-purpose cleaner, and a sleeve of paper cups. I don't think any of that stuff is going to help my head.

Slowly, I drag myself upward, using the sink, towel rack, anything to help. My head pounds, but I try to ignore it. I fumble at the door and swing it open.

The room outside is empty.

"Shit," I say. If Torden had gone to sleep, he'd be on the couch.

No one is on the couch.

I stagger forward.

The small table near the kitchen looks like two people ate and got up, with no concern for cleaning. Half of my salad remains, while Torden's plate is clear of everything except a dark, red liquid pooled around the well-gnawed bones of his lamb.

"Shit!" I say again.

I twist around, but what's the use? He's gone.

As if it will help, I scan the table. Next to Torden's empty glass tumbler is a small paper cup.

Was that there before? I think. I can't recall. But — crap, I've seen that kind of cup before. I lurch back into the bathroom, reach down, and throw open the cabinet door.

A sleeve of paper cups.

Next to the all-purpose cleaner.

"Son of a bitch," I mutter. I snatch up the cleaner and spin it around so I can see the back. Most of it's in French, which is useless for me, but a few things are printed in multiple languages, including English. Thankfully, the warning label is one of these things.

Keep out of reach of children. Avoid contact with skin. Eye irritant. If swallowed, may cause nausea, vomiting...

Even if it wasn't listed in English, there's a helpful little icon of a person's head, mouth open, guzzling the cleaner. All of this is surrounded by a red circle and crossed with a diagonal red line. You know, all the ways they can think of to say *Don't drink this!*

I scan the warning again, just to make doubly sure the stuff isn't lethal, because I definitely feel like I want to die. The language is a little vague on that point, ending instead with "*Call a doctor immediately.*" I don't have time for that. I head to the front door as my body shudders with a grotesquely liquid gurgle. As if I didn't have enough evidence already that Torden poisoned me and escaped, he kindly left my key in the lock, the final proof.

I shout curse words and pull the door open roughly, slamming it hard against the interior wall. I don't care. I stagger outside to stand on the little balcony, quickly scanning the streets below. I'm not high enough to see far, though. The only things I notice are empty, dark streets. Motion catches my attention, but it's only a solitary cat, meandering down the alleyway on my left, mocking me.

Going down to street level, I would have to start making choices about which way to go — left or right, toward the lake or away — and any decision I make will just be arbitrary. I decide to get higher instead.

Signore Bernasconi's building is six stories tall, with a communal patio on the roof that is mostly unused. I head for that, trying to see farther.

One of the primary aftereffects of barfing up everything I've ever eaten is a distinct lack of energy. Combine that with the fact that I feel like I've been hit by a truck, and it takes several eternities for me to reach the roof. From there, I can see pretty far, even catch a glimpse of the lake itself, its waters reflecting the clear night sky and a thousand twinkling stars.

I ride the railing along all four sides, straining my vision outward and down, looking for any sign of wispy white hair or a tan jacket. Or just movement. Any movement. Nothing.

How long has he been gone? The truth is, I have no idea. It could be hours, but even if it's only been a few minutes, the likelihood of Torden conveniently walking where I can see him seems slim.

"Damn it!" I slam the railing hard, succeeding mainly in hurting my hand. That makes me even more angry. "Damn it, Torden, you bastard! Now what am I supposed to do?"

I'm frustrated, furious, and half-dead from ingesting detergent. Apparently, in that sort of state, a person can make unwise decisions.

Though it does nobody any good, I raise my hands and fire a thick bolt of electricity at the sky, the sharp crackling sound it makes serving as a brash contrast to the far-too-quiet night. Geneva evenings aren't the cacophony of sound I'm used to from New York, at least not in this neighborhood.

A dog barks, startled by what I've done, then several others join the chorus. Lights go on in a nearby window, and someone pushes aside the drapes to look out. Other windows spring to life. *Now you've done it,* I think.

I duck down and head toward the stairs, trying to avoid notice. Well, trying to avoid *additional* notice. By the time I reach my flat's level, I hear voices from several directions, and though they aren't speaking English, I don't need a translation to understand what they're suddenly talking about. As I push my front door closed, a final look upward makes me want to kick myself.

There isn't a cloud in the sky.

11

THE TICKING CLOCK

"Good morning, Lyn. Where's your friend?" Signore Bernasconi says as he idly strokes one wrinkled hand along Pazzo's black fur. Signore sits outside his ground-floor flat in a little folding chair, despite the chill in the morning's air. Maybe the cat in his lap provides some bit of warmth. For his part, Pazzo has the appearance of a cat who's tolerating human attention, mostly because walking away would be too much effort.

"He had to leave sooner than expected," I say, not really much of a lie.

Signore squints, like he's trying to see me more clearly. "Are you okay, young lady? You look very pale this morning."

That noticeable, huh? Great. "I'm fine. I just, um, ate something last night that didn't agree with my stomach." Also not much of a lie.

He nods, apparently willing to accept both of my modified stories. "Quite a commotion last night." I stop, suddenly unsure how to respond. Had he seen something? Seen me? Thankfully, Signore continues without me having to ask. "Big crack and flash, very strange."

I decide to play dumb. "I must have been sleeping. What was it?"

Signore shrugs, and it's just enough movement to convince Pazzo finally to jump down and scurry away. "My friend Fritz lives just behind the building. He says he was sitting on his balcony late at night when lightning struck, out of nowhere. No storm clouds, no rain, just a bolt out of the blue, as they say. Or I suppose it was a bolt out of the black, given the time."

"Weird," I say, hoping my voice sounds more bored than tense.

"I'm not sure, though." He tilts his head and gives a knowing smirk.

Oh shit. He must have seen me. I try to keep my expression flat and my demeanor calm. "Why not? What do you think it was?"

"Well, you know, lightning doesn't just *appear* from nothing." His tone of voice is either very European or very coy, and I can't tell the difference. I swallow, hard, pissed for letting myself act so stupidly, and wondering how the hell I'm going to fix things if this old man, friendly though he is, saw what I can do. "No, I think it was something else entirely..."

"W— what?" I ask.

"Most likely a transformer exploding, or something like that, even though we didn't lose power. Still, that's more believable than Fritz's story. Lightning on a clear day? Ridiculous. Plus, I know Fritz. If he was sitting out on his balcony late at night, there was a glass of red wine in his hand, and it probably wasn't his first." Signore waggles his eyebrows in a knowing way, and I eject a brief stream of frail laughter that feels so heavy with worry it falls to the ground like spilled wine.

I STAND in front of Geneva's silly flower clock, surrounded by people. And yes, I know there are thousands of watchmakers in the city, and some of the most famous — and expensive — brands. But I'm talking about a basic clock mechanism buried in the dirt and littered with flowers and shrubbery. You want to impress me with intricately created timepieces, made of rose gold, painstakingly engraved, where the inner workings can be seen infinitely twisting and ticking away their microscopic motions? Fine. I'm impressed. Flower clock? Not so much.

I realize I've bashed the flower clock twice now. Apologies to Geneva, as neither of my visits to the clock were on what I would call my best day.

I did my best to parrot what Torden had broadcast. *This is Lyn Hopkins. I've come to Geneva because I want to arrange an audience with the.. Officials.* Yes, I stammer over calling my parents such a strange name, but given how distant — scratch that, nonexistent — our relationship has been over the years, I suppose it's as good a name as any.

No reply. Fine. I'm not expecting one. Torden didn't get one right away when he made the same announcement. I look at the clock on my phone, knowing full well there is a giant, silly clock sitting just next to me. It's a minute before noon.

I'm already standing in Jardin Anglais, waiting, and it's noon. I figured I'd get this part out of the way to speed things along. Torden told me repeatedly that there was a process, and if step two was "Meet by the big dumb clock," I was ready.

———

MY STOMACH GROWLS, which is just annoying. Sure, it's approaching dinner time and I'm still in the park, and sure, I skipped lunch. (Also, sure, breakfast was nothing more than half of a coffee, given the state of my digestive tract thanks to Torden Detonde.) I'm hungry but wary of eating too much for fear of a renewed bout of unswallowing. But what's the point of sitting here on a park bench as the day grows old and the temperature drops?

I stand up and immediately get the sense of being watched. I turn around slowly, scanning the nearby people. Sure enough, one person is looking right at me: a young man with smooth, dark skin wearing skinny black jeans and a trendy winter jacket, standing on the far side of the flower clock. His expression is mostly flat with a tinge of something else... pity? *Shit.*

I'm Lyn Hopkins, I say through static, broadcasting for any EM to hear.

Immediately, he responds in my head. *I know who you are. We all do. Go home, Lyn Hopkins. This is pointless.*

No, I say. *I need to see my parents. The, uh, Officials.*

You can't, he snaps back, still just staring at me from where he stands.

Why?

That's not for me to say.

Then there's no good reason. Show me the way to get to them.

He laughs. *I'm not that stupid.*

Well, you're talking to me now. If I'm not supposed to be here, I guess that makes you kinda stupid.

The man's expression darkens as his brow furrows. *I've ticked him off*, I think. Good. Maybe that will make him do something he isn't supposed to do.

Do you want to know what's stupid? Using your power where people can see you, and for no good reason. Do you think news of your little show last night went unnoticed? Sure, the regulars explain it away with their rationalizations, but how long until you do something they can't explain? How long until you expose us all?

I thought that's what the Prime Order wanted to do, I say, thinking myself pretty smart and witty with the comeback.

Only when we are ready. Not before. And not because some foolish young woman got tricked.

Damn it. That means they know all about Torden's escape. My momentary pride turns into self-doubt, and in a very real sense it's feels like a homecoming. Welcome back, misery. I knew you wouldn't stay away for long. *I wasn't tricked*, I say, though I know now how I sound saying it. Like some foolish little kid.

Instead of debating the point, the man looks to one side, sees the light change, and works into the crowd crossing the street. I hop up from the park bench. *Don't bother trailing me*, he says, not even looking back. *I'm going to dinner, then I'm going home. I haven't seen your parents in person in months, and I can easily go many more months without doing so again. Keep a watch on me, if you like. You'll just waste your time.*

Tragically, I believe him, letting the only possible connection to my parents simply walk away.

Someone taps me on the shoulder, and I turn around in a mild rage, startling a thirty-something, pasty-faced father with his wife and two kids standing near the flower clock. He pulls back, an apologetic smile on his face. The others look pleasant enough, though nondescript. Everyone's smiling, except me. "Sorry to bother you," he says with a jovial English accent. I realize that my entire conversation with that other EM was in our heads, so of course, to this guy, I just look like some tourist in the park. "Would you mind taking our photograph?" He holds out his phone, already set to the camera.

Ugh. "Sure," I say, taking it from him, probably a little too dramatically. "Where do you want it?"

The man screws up his face, looking at me sideways, before jerking a thumb toward his family, who arrange themselves in a group pose. "Front of the clock, of course."

The lake is steps away. Mountains circle in the distance. But everyone wants a photo of this damned thing. "Of course," I repeat, watching the giant second hand of the flower clock sweep along, time I'll never get back.

12

RADIO FREE EUROPE

A familiar voice buzzes in my head. *Lyn? You there?*

Zee? I reply groggily. Based on the sunlight streaming in bands through my window, I'd guess it's after noon, but I'm just waking up. When you walk the streets until the sky starts to lighten in the east, you're on a different schedule than most people. Raymond had to kick me out when he closed the bar, but I was nowhere near ready for sleep.

Lyn! Zee says excitedly. *Where are you?*

Oh shit. I thought I was dreaming, but this is happening. Zee's somewhere nearby, really speaking to me. Not just some idea rattling around in my sleeping brain. *Um, hi?* I rub my eyes. *What are you doing here?*

Your brother sent us, she says. *Where are you?*

I ignore the question. *Us?*

Pers is with me.

Okay, okay. I mean, it makes sense. They still work for Kevin, and they're a team. So, given that I kidnapped a prisoner of the High Order, I assume they're here to arrest me. My brother sent my friends to bring me in. Perfect. I play coy. *Why are you here?*

Yeah, have you not seen the news?

I have no idea what you're talking about, I reply. I have a bad feeling she's about to enlighten me.

Tell me where you are so we can come and talk, Zee says, a burst of static punctuating her statement.

I'm not going back with you. Even if you arrest me or try to force me. And Torden escaped, so you can't even take him back, either.

Arrest you? Do you think Pers or I would arrest you, even if we were given the order to do so? Do you really think that little of us?

No, I don't. I think a lot of them. And I miss having someone to call friend. I give her the address.

Minutes later, not only have Zee and Pers come to meet me at my flat, they've also shown me an online video of lightning shooting up from among the buildings of Geneva, from multiple angles and with multiple voiceovers describing what clearly must have happened. Thankfully, none of them are close enough to see me, just the bolt I produced.

They do, however, go on and on, applying random batshit crazy science. Please. The fact that my lightning took 2 seconds to produce and one of the commentary videos about it had a run time of nearly 10 minutes? That should tell you all you need to know.

"Okay, I kinda lost my cool, but at least no one can tell from the video that a person made that bolt of lightning." I scan their faces quickly, hoping they accept what was obviously a lame apology. "So you're here for that, and not for the whole Torden thing?"

"No, we're here for both," Percival says calmly. "Kevin is not happy about either. He wants to talk to you. And... I think he feels really bad about all the lying, about your parents."

"Well, he should."

"Still, I don't think he's going to say that makes what you did okay."

Ugh, fine. "Well, then, now what? You're not going to arrest me,

Torden got away, my parents won't see me, and Kevin's mad even though he lied to me for years."

Zee puts her hand on top of mine. "Lyn, we're your friends. You may not want to be part of what we're doing with the High Order anymore, but that doesn't make us stop being friends."

"I know," I say sheepishly, staring at the table between us. "Look, I'm sorry about how I've acted toward you all, disappearing, reappearing, giving you shit about the work you're doing. I hope you know it's not *you guys* that I'm really mad at."

"We know," Zee says.

Pers nods. "So let us help you."

I look up in shock. "*Help* me? You've gotta be kidding."

"Nope," he says. Now Zee's shaking her head. They mean it.

"You all will lose your jobs, or worse. Wouldn't that make you an accomplice, or in violation of some High Order rules? You can't risk that just for my little quest."

Their expressions turn gravely serious. "You risked your life to come to my rescue at Torden's pavilion," Percival says.

"And again when you thought you were avenging my death," says Zee.

"Besides," Pers adds with a grin. "I can always go back to doing odd jobs."

I pull back. "Absolutely not! I don't even know what those *odd jobs* entailed, but I doubt it was anything good." I sound like I'm scolding him or acting like his mother. Yeah, I'm sure everyone thinks that's super weird coming out of my mouth.

"True, many of them were, well, if not illegal, at least questionable."

Zee waves her hands. "None of that. You don't need to go back to sketchy life of crime or whatever it was, because we aren't going to lose our jobs. And Lyn, you're not going to be punished by the High Order."

"How can you be so sure?"

"Because that's why we're really here. Just to locate you. Think of us as the advance scout team."

"Um, I don't think I like the sound of that at all," I say with a little twitch. "If you're the advance team, who's coming here after you?"

Now it's Percival's turn to take my hand. "Listen, don't freak out. Kevin is coming. We just had to find where you were so that he can come directly to us all when he arrives. Tomorrow morning."

"We talked to him — a lot," Zee says. "Pers and I can be *persuasive* when we want to. So he came around."

"Came around? What are you talking about?"

Zee leans across the table, speaking in a calm, low voice. "He's going to take you to your parents."

There's a loud thump that I think may be my jaw hitting the floor.

13

BE CAREFUL WHAT YOU WISH FOR

"Hi," Kevin said, as if that made up for anything.

"Hi," I replied, as if that made up for anything. *Shit, families can be a pain in the ass.* "So, are we really doing this?" I ask.

He nods. Behind him, Zee and Pers let out the breath they were holding, probably unsure he was really going to go through with it until this very moment.

"Why did you lie to me for so long?"

Kevin sighs. "I truly believe that Mom and Dad have good reasons."

Truly believe? Why did he say truly believe? He doesn't know *what their reasons are?* I decide to hold off on asking that doozy of a question and try something else instead. "But why did *you* lie?"

His expression hardens. "Why did you break Torden out of the secured room where I had him held?"

Okay, fine, touché. Now I don't even know where to take the conversation. "Well, um, what do we do now?"

"I have a car coming. Under five minutes," he says. When it arrives, black, long, and sleek, I think it's just about the polar opposite from any typical European car. And, yeah, those were an awkward four-plus minutes.

———

I PACK UP ALL my things, which isn't a lot, then give Signore Bernasconi a smile, thank you, and a brief hug, before scratching the fur atop Pazzo's head. The cat, ever a cat, wanders away like none of this matters. I tell Signore a white lie — that my brother and friends have come and we're going to tour around the area before heading back to the States. He rents a flat in a popular European city. I'm certain this isn't his first or last goodbye to a tenant, though I imagine I stayed longer than most. Maybe he's sad to see me go because he's actually grown some fondness for me. The jaded side of me wonders if he's sad because a constant income stream suddenly dried up.

Gazing out the window from the back of Kevin's car as we roll along for many kilometers, I realize it's no wonder I never found my parents in Geneva. Technically, they don't live there. We glide in that unnaturally bump-free way luxury cars do, along the lakeside for some time, heading north, before the driver turns left and heads up a hill.

There's a gate. Not surprisingly, it's guarded. Our driver defers to Kevin, who briefly slides his window down, then up. His face seems to be enough. They let us in. We crunch over the gravel drive toward a house that looks like a castle, light yellow in color, the structure wrapping around the drive on three sides, U-shaped. The driver pulls to the middle, stops, and someone opens the door.

I have to be dreaming.

Someone offers me a hand, but I decline. I stand. I look around.

Back the way we came, there's a wide yard with a dozen or more people standing around for no apparent reason. All of them are staring at us, some openly with disbelief.

Thankfully, I'm not the only one staring back at them; Zee and Pers are sharing my amazement. I mean, come on, none of us have lived in a European palace before. None of us have even visited one.

Despite my family's wealth, my parents left before this kind of posh location could serve as a sort of vacation destination for us. And I used all of my air travel since then to charge hunt.

"This must be... a haven for EMs. Like Torden's pavilion," I say. "Only way fancier."

Kevin looks around quickly, familiar yet wistful. "This is so much more than anything Torden ever did." He gestures for me to follow him inside, and we head toward the oversized front door.

Before we get to it, the door opens and two people step out into the sunlight. Though they're who I've been seeking for so long, who I know we're here to see, it's more than surreal to behold my parents standing *right there*.

I stop, catching my breath. Suddenly, now, it's happening.

They look... old. I guess that's to be expected. I haven't laid eyes on them in twenty years.

I've had so many dreams about them that seeing them in person feels like a dream. I blink. They're still there. Plus, in my dreams, it's usually been the younger version of them, the age they were before they disappeared from my life. The age they are in those last pictures around the house, photos I only now realize just how much I treasure. And only now I realize how much those photos have lied to me about what they truly look like today. Even the occasional dream where I imagined them at their correct age had it wrong in many ways.

"Mom? Dad?" I say. "Why?" It's the simplest question, but encompassed all of my thoughts.

Jeremy Hopkins, my father, stands in pressed slacks and a neat blue buttoned-up shirt. His full head of hair is a mixture of blond and grey, much thinner than in my memory. Mom — Marianne — wears an understated pair of brown slacks and a white blouse topped by a sweater to ward her from the cool weather. Her short, dark hair shows they grey much more than Dad's, from her temples down, encircling her face. Neither has that unnaturally preserved look Torden has to his skin, which would be a relief if it weren't for the way they're looking at me; they both wear completely unreadable expressions.

"Welcome to our chateau. Please come inside, Lyn," my father says. "We have a lot to talk about."

Well, that's a freaking understatement.

———

I DON'T KNOW why I'm at first surprised to see there are servants, but I am. Many. And I'm pretty sure they're regular humans, too. Which is completely in keeping with Juliet, back home, so again, not sure why I'm surprised, but I guess having all the pieces of your life suddenly align around you can be a little disconcerting.

So my parents have regular humans around, and they are openly and obviously electromagicians. This is completely at odds with everything I ever heard through my loose connections with the High Order, but of course lines up neatly with what I know about the Prime Order. You know, the group my parents apparently founded.

"We'll use *le petit salon*," my father says, and a butler nods briskly before dashing off to prepare something. I can't help but gawk at the high, vaulted ceilings as we walk down the corridor, even though, you know, I live in a mansion in downtown Manhattan. Compared to our home, this place screams Old World Rich, and that's a different beast, I can assure you. Manhattan, as a city, is what? A few hundred years old? This place looks like kings and queens used to roam its halls, not stockbrokers and real estate magnates.

When we arrive at a room large enough to have four distinctly different sitting areas, my father gestures toward one of the tables. *Oh, so this is the* petit *salon. Of course.* Every inch of the walls and ceiling has been painted with faux columns and classical figures, like a Renaissance masterpiece in all directions. Lush red drapes line the windows and even cover a side door, no doubt where a butler will soon emerge. Wouldn't want the rich to be bothered to see the servants' entrance.

I sit. We all do. And I realize, unbelievably, that my family is all here, in one place, back together again for the first time in decades. Something about it tickles the back of my mind, maybe a memory from long ago. Did we sit like this for meals when I was a kid? We must have. My memory's just too fuzzy.

There's something else, too. A strange sort of tingling sensation all over my body, like my EM powers are... I don't know how to put it. Like they're *paying attention*. It's making this weird situation even more weird.

Because that's on top of the fact that I am feeling every single emotion at the same time. Joy, love, relief, frustration, anger, sadness, remorse. It makes me speechless.

As I try to gain control of myself, I simply scan left to right. Six chairs around the table, six of us. Convenient. I take a deep breath. Sitting next to me is my mother, which I honestly can't believe is happening. Next is my father, then Kevin, Pers, and finally Zee, in the seat directly to my right. Everyone stares. No one says anything.

Thankfully, my mother breaks the silence. She starts to reach out a hand for me, then thinks better of it — maybe she feels she hasn't earned that privilege. I don't know. I mean, I don't know either way. I don't know if she's thinking that, and I don't know if I'd let her. "Lyn. I — *we* are so very sorry. And so very glad to see you after all this time. You look so..." Her voice breaks slightly, then she continues with a sad smile. "...grown up. You're a beautiful young woman now. I just hope that you try to understand that it was meant to be for your own good. For the good of all."

Well, that's a phrase that doesn't alleviate my emotions or speech-lessness. *For the good of all?* My parents hiding from me, and even making me believe they might be dead, was for the good of all? I don't understand the world at all. And so that's all I can think of to say. "I don't understand."

My father looks at the table, as if for answers or maybe just a hint at where to start. "The only way this is going to work is if we start at the beginning. Do you know the Oath of the High Order?"

That's an unexpected question. "Yeah... Yes — I mean, well, *no*. Not really." The actual truth is that I have no clue what it says. I just don't like looking stupid. "I generally understand what it's about, but I don't have it memorized or anything."

Kevin speaks. "I do. And it's important. Because the Oath is why we've been separated for so long. And why we'll have to be separated again."

"That makes no sense," I say. "Why?"

"Let me recite the Oath to you first, then we can go on." And so he does.

14

THE OATH OF THE HIGH ORDER

I, (state your name), hereby enter the High Order as a/n (state your incoming rank; if not previously determined otherwise, say "initiate") member in its ranks, and all the benefits and privileges provided to such a member, contingent upon my acceptance and adherence, without question, to the following regulations:

I will not cause the death or injury of another member of the High Order, whether intentional or otherwise;

I will not reveal the existence of the High Order or electromagicians in general to any regular human or any entity of regular human government, industry, or community;

I will not, without explicit permission, affect, claim, take, or otherwise manipulate the electromagnetic power of any individual or group;

I will not use my electromagnetic power for personal gain or at the expense of others;

I will not act against the will of the High Order, its officials, or its members;

I will respect the hierarchy of membership in the High Order and follow the instruction of my elders and superiors;

I recognize and submit to my local High Order district of (state your district here), and will abide by the policies, judgments, and other doctrines *of (state the name of your district leader here) as well as any future leaders appointed;*

If I visit a district of the High Order other than my own, at all times I recognize and submit to that district and its leader, and, if there is a discrepancy between the policies of the districts, I agree to abide by the policies of the district in which I am physically located at the time of any event in question;

I recognize and submit to the judgment of the elders of the High Order as the final decision makers for any policies, doctrines, determinations of violation, punishments, or other matters related to any and all electromagician affairs.

If I am found in violation of this Oath, I submit to all necessary judgments or punishments, including but not limited to expulsion from the High Order, confinement, and/or the permanent removal of my electromagic abilities.

Effective this date of (state the date) and continuing for the duration of my life span, I, (state your name), hereby swear.

PART II

A VAST PRACTICAL JOKE

15

DIVIDED BY WORDS

"Okay, so now what?" I ask, moments after my brother finishes reciting the Oath of the High Order. "I mean, haven't you violated at least one of those, Kevin?"

"What do you mean?"

"Revealing the existence of EMs. Or did you forget that Juliet works for you?"

"She works for us," my father says. "And we are no longer in the High Order. And while she is a regular human and is aware of our special abilities, that knowledge came from me, not from Kevin."

"That seems like splitting hairs."

Kevin just nods. "I understand there's very little distinction. But not once in my life have I ever demonstrated ability in front of her, nor have I discussed electromagicians with her in any way. So, while it seems like a technicality, I haven't violated my oath. And yes, I realize that I'm the only one at this table who still adheres to the Oath."

"I never took it," I say.

"But we did," my mother replies. "And then we broke it, so we had to leave. That was the start of our rift. The start of us creating the Prime Order."

"With Orkan?" I ask.

"Yes," my father says. "There were others as well, people dissatisfied with the positions of the High Order, looking for more."

"You mean, to be able to integrate fully into society with regulars?"

My father sighs. "One day, yes."

It's all stuff I've been told before, here and there, one way or another. "Okay, but none of that explains your absence. I was a *kid* —"

My mother reached out, and this time her hands do cover mine on the table. "I know it was hard for you. Please believe that it was so, so *very* hard for us, as well. For me."

I want to believe her — I mean, who doesn't want to believe that their parents care for them? — but still, there's been nothing said to explain the whole thing. "Tell me now. There is a reason for all this, and I need to know now, or I'll go nuts, or scream, or maybe just leave and convince myself you actually are dead. I'm here, and it's time."

My father glances around the table. "It's almost time. But there's one thing first. Kevin?"

My brother slides back his chair and stands. "If you'll excuse me, I have a plane to catch back to New York."

I lurch forward, over the table at him. "What? After all this time, and you're just leaving? Why? Because you've known the reason all along and never told me?" I'm suddenly furious at Kevin, even though he flew across the ocean, drove me to my parents, and now is about to fly back, all in 24 hours.

Pushing his chair back in, Kevin puts his hands on the back of the seat and droops. He looks tired, maybe beaten. Finally, he raises his eyes to meet mine. In that gaze, I see sorrow, and something else. What? Not fear. Not Kevin. No way. He sighs. "Lyn, I'm sorry. I love you, my sister, and I know there *is* a reason. But that's all I know."

My father interjects. "Kevin knows that the reason for our self-imposed exile is exactly why he has to leave, and nothing more. If he hears what we say to you today, he will be breaking his oath and subject to the rules of the High Order. He would lose everything."

"Not everything!" I shout. "He could still live in *your* house. He wouldn't be penniless and on the street."

"But I would lose my life and my job and my integrity. I know that not everyone can understand the High Order, but it's my life, and I like it. That's all I can say about it." He releases the seat back and stands up straight.

Suddenly, I'm looking at my brother not as a pain in the ass sibling, a rule enforcer, or someone who's kept me in the dark. I'm looking at him as a person, with his own wants and needs. He's not me. Nothing in this world says he has to want what I want or do what I say. I... Strangely, I respect that. I lean back into my chair and nod to him, enough that he and I understand each other. He turns, and I hear the hard heels of Kevin's dress shoes clack over the wooden floor as he walks to the door and leaves the room.

Percival, nervously, raises a hand, like a kid in third grade. When my parents look at him in curiosity, he speaks, but it's not in his typical charming and self-assured way. He sounds tentative, concerned. "Um, hi. My name is Percival Farimir, sir. Ma'am." Pers gestures toward Zee. "My friend — uh, colleague — here, Miss Mackenzie Patmina, and I have, um, also taken the oath of the High Order."

"You did?" I stammer, looking back and forth between them.

Zee shrugs. "After we got back from Paris, your brother invited us to make our roles more formal."

"I can't believe it..." I say. "Why didn't he make you go with him?"

Scoffing, Zee gives me a sidelong glance. "He said if he did what we wanted — bring you here — we have to be responsible for our own actions once things started to happen. We didn't really know what that meant, so we said sure. It isn't like we knew this was gonna get all political and shit."

My mother leans forward, speaking in a calm voice. "Mackenzie. Percival. We know you both very well. As Lyn's friends, we have taken an interest in following your lives, to the degree we can, from afar. And we understand that you also have taken the Oath. You have three options. You can either leave for New York, with Kevin, or stay here, but leave the room. If you stay, you're welcome to explore the grounds, or, if you're tired, we have rooms prepared." She gives a look to my father. "We always have rooms prepared for visitors." Yeah, it really is like a posh version of Torden's pavilion. "But if you wish to hear what we're about to say, your only other option is to leave the High Order and join us in the Prime Order."

Percival pipes up, giving an almost involuntary twist to his neck. "Ma'am. Sir. We, uh, just recently arrived in your fair land of Europe, so going home now seems... wrong." I'm not sure the continent has ever been referred to as the *fair land of Europe* before, but Pers seems earnest enough that offering a correction would be unkind. Plus, he won't look at me, and seems to be blushing. "I honestly can't say I know enough about the Prime Order to just jump ship, though the High Order has been mostly just a job for me. But, if you don't mind me saying so, I think it's best that you talk to your daughter in private, at least for now. Personally, I'm okay with figuring out where I end up with all this later on. So, I would prefer to leave the room, take a look around the grounds maybe, then have a little rest. Zee?"

Mackenzie thinks about it all for a moment, then nods. "He's right. You should talk to Lyn alone first. She's been waiting a really long time to understand what happened. First and foremost, it's between you and your family. Telling us can wait." She pushes back her chair and a moment later they walk out the same door where Kevin left, leaving me alone for the first time in more years than I can remember with my parents, two people I thought were dead.

16

ALL THERE IS TO KNOW

"The first thing you need to know is that your mother and I are extremely powerful electromagicians. As are you. Your brother is strong, of course, but we three are... well, let's just say we're in the top one percent of all EMs ever born. And that's important, because the difference in power for electromagicians is *exponential*. Those of us at the very top of the scale are approximately twice as capable with electromagic as those only one level below. So, while Kevin is quite high on the chart as well, the difference between *him* and *you* — or *us* — is, let's say, somewhat extreme."

I pull back. The first part of what he says strikes me as arrogance, but the last part? I mean, sure, I *feel* like I'm strong, and I know Torden ranked me at the top of his own stupid scale — along with himself — but top one percent ever? Exponentially higher than my own brother? Besides... scales? Sounds a lot like Torden speaking, and that is not a comfortable thought.

"Wow," I say. Nothing more eloquent comes to mind. "But what difference does that make? I mean, I'm still just me, and it isn't like EM power can, I don't know, make me a top chef or earn me a wonderful income. What's the point of it, and what does it matter that I might be able to do more than someone else? What would I even *do*?"

"The information we've given you so far, including Kevin reciting the Oath of the High Order, is simply setting the stage for what you really need to know," my father says.

I sigh audibly with frustration. "Could we just cut to the chase?" I've been separated from my parents for about two decades. Now they're in a room with me, and no one else is around. I'm edgy to make up for lost time. Or at least figure out what the hell is going on.

My mother clears her throat. "That's not quite as easy to do as it might seem. But it starts with your extreme power."

"Do you mean Quotient, or something else?"

"Everything is intertwined," my father says. "Your Quotient, which is essentially the ability for you to stretch the use of any charge you have, is extraordinarily high, but so is your ability to store a charge."

"Like, I have a deep well?" It's the best analogy I can think of.

"That's a reasonable way to put it. And in addition to your ability to stretch your charge and store a lot of it, you also have the capability to focus your use of electromagic much more than the average EM."

"Really?" I ask. "I don't notice any difference. The times I've seen others fire off a bolt of energy, it looks pretty much exactly like my own."

"Informally, that might be true. But when you were little, we did measurements. We tested your output, so to speak. And the difference was clear. But I can understand that from your perspective, your abilities simply feel... *natural*."

It's a lot to take in, and I look down at the table as if it might give me clarity. It doesn't. "Hold on a second. You... tested my output? When I was little?"

Mom replies defensively, quickly trying to dispel the strangeness of the idea. "It was nothing harmful to you, Lyn. We simply asked you to shoot a bolt of your energy into a machine that took a reading. It's not like you were strapped to an examination table or anything like that." At least she has the decency to look embarrassed.

"Okay, and so still the question is... who cares?"

My father sighs. "It isn't the Quotient, or the *well*, as you call it, or the intensity of your power. Those are just things you need to understand first. What matters is what happens when you're *near* someone else with a similar level of power."

Now it's my turn to sigh, but mine comes out distinctly more annoyed. "Look, I already know that when I'm near another EM, I can feel and use their well of power, and they can, too. That's not exactly news, and hardly seems like enough reason to hide from your daughter for twenty years."

My mother nods sympathetically. "All true. And you can do that with *any* electromagician. But we're talking about when you're near someone with the highest level of power. People like us. Can you *feel* us? Feel our power, right here in front of you, right now?"

"Uh," I stammer. "I don't know. I'm not really trying."

"Try," she says with a heavy expression. She looks at me as if something terrible may be about to happen. Or maybe she looks at me like it *won't*, and that the real terrible thing is that they left me so long ago.

I'm not even sure how to begin, but I close my eyes and reach inside to feel my own electromagic.

And then I gasp. There's something else there. No, two other things.

"You can, can't you?" she asks.

I don't have words, but I nod. Then slowly I open my eyes.

My parents both dip their chins, a gesture that seems to indicate both their regrets and my lack of understanding. "Lyn, it's more than just an ability to sense us, it's much more. If we were near you over these last twenty years — years when you were growing, not fully able to understand and use your power... Not mature enough..." Ouch. "Things could have happened. Things you wouldn't necessarily have wanted to happen, but because of your age and inexperience, they might have happened anyway."

"Like what?" I throw up my hands, so confused and pissed off.

"You might have —" my mother begins.

My father interrupts. "You might have killed someone. You might have destroyed half of New York City for all we really know. You might have done anything." He's not yelling or preaching, just stating facts. Facts that sound like insanity to me.

Mom hangs her head. "Even if, in your heart, you thought you were doing something good."

"What does that mean?" I ask. Then it strikes me all at once. Something happened. There *must* have been something that happened. Some *catalyst*. "Oh God. What did I do?" What did I do that made it clear to my own parents that they had to run away from me? Hide and pretend to be dead for two decades, all the years when I was growing up and truly needed parents in my daily life?

"You..." My father trails off.

"Just tell me!" I shout, standing.

I expect my father to be the one to say it, but instead it's my mother, bursting out the words like finally she can shed some massive weight from her shoulders. "You did something none of us could have ever expected. You created them — Percival and Macken-zie. Your friends..." She starts to cry.

"What the hell are you talking about?" I say, stunned. "I can't... *create*... people..." *Can I?*

Dad waves his hands before wrapping one arm around Mom to console her. "No, no, of course not. You didn't make them out of thin air or anything like that. But... you changed them. Please. Sit down."

I flop into the chair again. "I *changed* Pers and Zee. What does that even mean?"

My father shakes with frustration. "I wish I knew how to explain it, but here are the facts. You, Percival, and Mackenzie have been friends since you were very little."

"I remember that much. I have flashes of memories. Us in elementary school, maybe even kindergarten."

"Right," he says, "but what you probably don't remember is that, back then, they were just regular humans."

My stomach seizes, bile pushes upward. I'm going to be sick. I know what he's trying to say immediately, and it's impossible. *No, no, no, no nonononononono!* "That can't be true."

"It is, Lyn," my mother says, trying to face me with the most compassionate expression she can.

Nothing helps. No words, no kindness. I put my hands to my head, tight. "You're telling me that I have some kind of crazy ability and turned my own *friends* into electromagicians? How? Why? Why would I do that?"

My father clears his throat and speaks softly. "You said you wanted friends who were *like you*."

"Oh my God," I say. "This is worse than anything I could have ever imagined. I'm..." I bark a harsh, bitter laugh, dropping my hands to my lap. "I'm a goddamned monster." I fumble out of the chair and run from the room, bursting down a long hallway, unsure where I'm going. But finally I find a door that leads me out into the light, gasping for air like I can never possibly get enough to breathe again.

17

REFLECTIONS

I run across the wide driveway, simply trying to get away from everyone, *everything*, and knowing full well that I spent years trying to get to my parents, only to want nothing of the sort anymore. So, of course, I run directly into Percival and Zee. Like, literally. I hit Pers so hard that he's forced to wrap his arms around me to keep us from both crashing to the gravel drive. My reaction to his touch is cruelly instinctive. God, I've missed this sensation.

"Hey, hey, Lyn! Slow down. What happened in there?" I push away from him despite it all. Or because of it all. Because of what I did. I stammer out a string of sounds that are unlikely to form any coherent words.

Zee raises a hand, gesturing for Percival to drop it. "Whatever she heard from them, remember that we're not supposed to hear it. Our oath, and all."

"She's clearly upset. And maybe I don't care too much about that oath anymore," he says.

I manage a single, sputtered word — "Sorry" — then sprint past them, toward a line of trees. *Sorry!* I scream at myself. *Well, that's an understatement. Sorry for ruining your entire lives, both of you, when I was supposed to be your friend. Sorry!*

There's a secluded little area in the middle of a stand of trees, and of-freaking-course there's a quaint reflecting pool in the center, with a bench on either side. I pick one and drop onto it with a dull thump.

Leaning forward, I can see my face reflected on the surface of the water, hardly a ripple distorting the view. It's poetic. Too poetic. Damn, I'm really sick of all this EM nonsense and wealth and perfectness that isn't really perfect at all. None of it is. Certainly not me. Everything that seems wonderful and perfect in my world is really just a mask over horrible, horrible things.

Something about *me* is so messed up that my own parents realized I couldn't be controlled, and the better option was to fly halfway around the world and hope I forgot they existed.

That's so incredibly screwed up.

Even still, I spent years wondering where they were. Years hoping I could see them again. And a month wandering a city looking for them, when my own brother knew where they were the whole time.

My friends pressed Kevin to ensure the whole thing happened, which made me so happy... until my parents told me the reason they couldn't be near me was because I *warped* my friends. Turned them from people into... *things like me.*

That's so colossally screwed up.

I'm so colossally screwed up.

Already slouched over, looking at my miserable face in reflection, I sink further until my head is firmly in my hands, and I cry.

Suddenly, there's a warmth on both of sides, as first Percival sits to my left and puts his arm over my shoulders, then Zee echoes him on my right, her arm around my waist. "Please, you guys..." I say, blubbering and ragged.

"There's no need to say anything," Pers says. From their body language, I can tell they're both refusing to leave me alone. So I let the tears continue to fall until eventually they dry up.

I breathe in and out, trying to calm myself enough to at least say thank you to my friends. Friends I don't deserve to have. Finally, I'm able to do it. "Thanks, guys. Sorry... for all of this." If they only knew what *all of this* really meant.

I lean back and Zee slips her arm out from behind me, moving her hand to my knee instead. "Hey. Whatever it is that they said, it's okay. We're still here for you."

I almost start to cry again at the tragic irony of what she's saying. *Maybe not if you knew what I know...*

Pers gives my shoulders a gentle squeeze. "And, you know, I can't speak for Zee, but if you want to get it off your chest and tell me what they said, I'm all ears. I'll help however I can." Then he leans in and whispers, like we're spies in a thriller, conspiring in the park, away from other ears. "Frankly, I'm not much of an oath-follower anyway, so I don't really care about that part. I've been a rebel, outsider EM all my life. Don't mind being one again."

"That's just it —" I blurt, then slam my jaw closed to shut myself up. *Me and my damned big mouth. Shut up, Lyn Hopkins!*

Pers leans back. "What?"

"What do you mean?" Mackenzie says, her voice drawn out. Like she's thinking.

Oh crap. I know Zee, and I know she's smart. Has she already figure it out — or enough of it — from just three words? I hope not.

"It has something to do with Percival?" she asks, and man, sometimes I wish I had dumber friends.

Shit, no, I think. *Don't wish for things!* This close to my parents, I'd better watch what I ask for. I might just give Zee an electromagic lobotomy. "No, of course not," I say, and I am the world's worst liar, so now they both completely know it has something to do with Percival.

"Does it have to do with me, too?" Zee asks, and again, I can't believe how I said almost nothing and she's made the exact two correct mental leaps.

My shoulders sink, and they both must know they've hit the nail on the head. Both nails on both heads. "Okay, look. Fine, it has something to do with you two, but I *can't* tell you. I can't be the one who screws up your oath like I screwed up —" *Oh my God! I need to wrap my face in duct tape. I literally can't stop saying things I shouldn't say!*

"Like you screwed up...?" Pers says, squinting his eyes and letting the words drift away. "Your parents left you for twenty years, and it has something to do with me and Zee, and something that you screwed up." He shakes his head once, quickly. "Well, that does it. To hell with any oath. Now I need to know what they said." He even smiles. At me. I look at his face and want to freeze time. If I tell Pers the whole truth, will he ever smile at me again? Zee, too, for that matter.

"Guys, I *can't* tell you. I just can't."

Zee pats my knee. "He's right. I don't give a damn about the oath either. If it's something that involves all three of us, I want to know about it."

"I can't."

"Please," she says, too warmly for what I deserve.

"No."

"Come on, Lyn," Pers urges. "We're your friends. We all been friends since before I can even remember. You can tell us anything. *Especially* this, whatever it is."

"No, please."

Zee leans in and fixes me with a compassionate look, and once more it's an expression I wonder if I'll ever see again, if I speak. "It can't be that bad. Like Pers says, we've been friends forever. The Three EM Amigos. From the start. To the end. It's okay, Lyn. Tell us."

I stand abruptly, swinging around to look at them both, tears once more welling in my eyes. Percival's smile. Zee's kind face. "It hasn't always been this way!" I blurt.

"What does that mean?" Mackenzie asks.

"I made you two! I turned you into EMs when we were little kids so I could have people like *me* to play with! You guys used to be... You used to be *regulars*." I immediately regret saying it as I watch both of their expressions fall. My heart shatters at the change.

Pers tilts his head, his smile gone. "That's... not possible."

"No," I bark. "Unfortunately, it is. At least for me. Apparently, my power, when I'm around other extremely powerful EMs — like either one of my parents — can do things no one really understands. You two were regular people — kids! — but that wasn't good enough for me, so somehow I changed you. You two became electromagicians because of me."

They stare at me, confusion and disbelief on the two faces that moments before looked at me with love.

Zee stands, slowly, deliberately. "I think, um, I need some time alone. To try to understand this." She turns and walks back to the house, and her back is like scorn to me.

"Yeah, so do I," Percival says, rising. "Sorry, Lyn. That's heavy shit. I've got to think about what this means." He turns away, too, but doesn't follow Zee. Instead, he wanders off somewhere else in the gardens.

Just like that, we are each alone, and I fear that alone is something I'll be for a long, long time.

18

BARBARIANS AT THE GATE

Alone, I walk the grounds of my parents' damned European palace overlooking Lake Geneva as the sun begins to set. I'm really not sure what I want to do. Passively accept it all and go to sleep in some posh and undeniably comfortable room in the mansion that looms over everything in the gardens, or just walk out the gate and never be a part of this life again?

I don't want to start over.

I love my friends.

I don't know what to think about Mom and Dad, or Kevin, but they're family, and not loving them and wanting their company, at least from time to time, is a hell of a lot harder than I thought it would be.

But Zee?

She's my closest friend. Basically my sister. Yeah, I somehow turned her into an EM and will forever have that guilt between us, but I would do anything for her. Especially now that I feel responsible for the mess I made of her life.

And Pers?

Do I love him?

I believe I do, and all the running away, trying to fix my own life, has just been a stalling tactic. I think I need to tell him how I feel, even if he rejects me and never wants to look at me again.

But do I deserve these friends? I'm near my parents, and that alone is sufficient to make me some kind of nuclear-blast-level unknown, from what I've been told. According to my own parents, anything might happen.

Could I make more EMs? My parents, Prime Order people who routinely work with regulars, have a number of armed, normal humans guarding the perimeter. Orkan had guards, too. But what are they all guarding? Was it guarding against... me?

Could I go off like a bomb? I don't even know what an electrobomb would look like. An EMP? The kind of pulse that kills everything electronic within a certain radius? That seems unlikely, but hey, what the hell do I know? Maybe I could self-correct. Blow up like an electromagnetic pulse and destroy myself along with every other EM, car radio, toaster, and computer in a ten-mile radius. I suppose it has to be on the list of "Possible Problems," since "Creating New EMs" is apparently on that list already, and I would never have assumed that could be true.

I turned Zee and Pers into EMs.

As Percival says, that's some heavy shit.

As I wander close to the front gate, guarded by four armed men, I hear a car approaching, and pause to watch out of curiosity.

The driver pushes a button to lower his window, calling out to one of the guards. "Hey, is that the old castle, up the drive?" he asks in English. *Tourist.*

"*Oui,*" the guard replies, unwilling to indulge the car full of strangers in their native language, though I assume he speaks fluent English. Basically, because he didn't have to ask for the question to be asked again in French.

The tourist driver grins. "Awesome! Can we tour it? I hear it's beautiful." Other voices in the car echo this sentiment. But... something feels off. Their words sound, I don't know... rehearsed?

"*La maison est privée,*" the guard says, and even I don't need a degree in French linguistics to understand that really means *piss off.*

There are a few more words, and the guard repeats his statement that the house is off limits to strangers. Then, something very unexpected happens.

Someone opens the rear passenger-side door and charges the gate. I'm so stunned by what I'm seeing, I freeze. It's a ropey guy who looks to be in his twenties, with shaggy dark hair that dangles down into his eyes as he runs. He's tall and skinny, but his midsection looks oddly thick.

Something splatters on my face, and I realize five things all at once: I'm on my ass in the grass, my ears are ringing, my vision is blotched by a large blind spot, the iron gate has been knocked off its hinges and is sitting at a strange angle, and the man who jumped out of the car is gone.

No. Not gone. *Mostly* gone.

That man — moments before a living, breathing human being around my age — is nothing but scraps of clothing and viscera. Wiping my forehead, my hand comes away streaked with red. My stomach lurches. I'm about to throw up.

Then more doors open on the car, and three other people, all young men, run toward the now-broken gate. Through it, past the stunned guards. Onto to the grounds, which means toward me.

I roll onto my feet, then duck behind a thick row of bushes and fill myself with electromagic energy, knowing full well that I can't stave off bullets or explosions.

My vision is still haloed from the brightness of the blast, and everything sounds muted, but even still, I can hear footsteps on the gravel, so close, then running past where I am and heading for the house.

Zee is in there.

Percival is in there.

My parents are in there.

I stand and step out from behind the bushes, readying myself to fire electricity into the backs of the intruders, knowing that, whoever they are, whatever they want, they shouldn't be here. I'm going to try to do it without killing them, mostly because I want answers.

I raise my hand to strike, blinking to try to see better.

Suddenly there's a series of muted pops through the ringing in my ears, like someone is bursting balloons in another room.

The three men drop to the ground, fresh red circles now dotting their clothes.

I realize the gate guards are standing to my left, and they each hold some sort of dangerous military-style rifle. And I realize that it's over now; the intruders are quickly bleeding to death on the gravel driveway. One of the armed guards walks toward them, still aiming his weapon.

And the young man in the middle rolls over, smiling through bloody teeth, grabbing at something on his chest.

"No! Stop!" I shout, instinctively turning away and ducking.

Then, for the second time in just minutes, there's a deafening explosion, and I can feel wet things spraying onto me, some thumping against me with a disturbingly solid feel. I'm vaguely glad the first blast screwed up my vision, because I definitely don't want to see clearly what's falling all around me now.

This time I can't help it, and everything I've eaten that day gets churned back up onto the red splattered grass. Then, I fall backward to sit roughly, confused and weary, one tiny figure in the middle of this insane scene of carnage.

19

A LIFE OF SECRETS

A hand touches my shoulder, and I pull away in shock.

"Lyn! Oh my God!" It's Zee. "Are you hurt? We need to get you to a hospital."

Except I'm not hurt. I'm covered in blood and... *other things...* but none of it is mine. My ears continue to ring and the blind spot in my vision is only slowly starting to fade. "No, I'm okay. I think."

She pulls back. "What the hell happened here?"

And that's the question, isn't it? What the hell did happen here? People are dead, and not in a tidy way at all. Looking around, I see that all three of the men who had been running for the house died in the blast, as did one of the guards. That's four, plus the one that took out the gate. Five very messy deaths. The smell is not something I want to think about or ever experience again. "I have no idea."

My parents emerge from their castle stronghold, shellshocked. Maybe it's not quite the stronghold they thought. And my dad, who I am desperately trying not to hate for leaving me alone to figure out a level of EM power even he couldn't understand, says something to me that does nothing to improve our relationship. "Did you tell anyone else you were coming here?"

Blood drips into my eyes, and angrily I flick it away with one hand. "You're asking if *I* did this? Me? How would that be even remotely possible? Until Kevin drove us all here, I had no idea where you were!"

"Sorry," he says, hands up, looking over the scene and trying to assess what to do next. He seems truly remorseful for asking the question, which I suppose is a plus. And I realize that it isn't just four strangers blown to bloody bits on his front lawn. The guard they took out with their last hurrah must have been someone my father knew.

"Lyn," Zee says, snapping me out of my daze. "I'm gonna leave."

I turn to look at her, but she won't meet my eyes. Still, what can I say? I just told her that the vast majority of her life was corrupted because I wanted a childhood plaything. My opinion is probably not going to be welcomed. "Um, okay."

"I'm gonna leave, and it's important for me to tell you why." I just nod. "You said you somehow changed me, and Percival, into electromagicians when we were all little kids, and since you don't even remember doing it, and I don't remember it happening, it seems almost dumb to be upset about it. But I am. It's made me realize things. You know, things like *this* —" She gestures to the horrors around us. "— have become all too frequent in my life, and if I had never been changed... Never become an EM, well..."

"I... I understand," I say, keenly aware that I'm still covered in the remains of several people. "Can I clean up first, then we can talk?"

"Actually, looking at you now is what forced me to make up my mind. Look around. These people are *dead*. We're at some mansion in Switzerland. I've been forced to hide most of my life from my own parents. I was almost blown to bits in Paris, and we've hunted down other electromagicians who've used their abilities to kill people we love. That I love. Like Hayden. And... Robin." Her voice cracks, saying his name. "And yet, we are — I am — expected to just *accept* this all as normal. But it isn't normal. And knowing what I know now, I have to wonder what else I might have been, or done. I feel like, I don't know, a lion in a zoo. Sure, there are things to like about the zoo, like they feed you and maybe you live longer, but you're not living the life you're supposed to live. That's me now. All of this stuff is completely insane, and I can't deal with it anymore, and the only reason I'm part of this at all is because of you."

The words burn into my heart, and I can't imagine I will ever forget them or ever forgive myself. *Because of you.* "I know it doesn't count for anything, Zee, but I'm so, so sorry. For everything I did and everything you've been through because of me."

My best friend doesn't smile, not really. It's more of a weak grimace feigning as a smile. But that's all she can manage before turning and quietly heading into the house.

20

ENTROPY

I shower a good twenty minutes, soaping and shampooing up multiple times to make sure I'm completely clean. As for my bloody clothes, I stuff them into a garbage bag and leave it outside my room, as requested by my mother. I don't know where that bag is taken, and frankly don't care, because I'm never putting on those things again. From my duffle, I rummage out a slightly crumpled black t-shirt and a pair of dark jeans, then slip into those and a grey jacket.

When I find my parents afterward, they're having words with Percival in the same ridiculously opulent room where we first sat.

"How many people do you have here, anyway?" Pers says.

"There are 62 electromagicians and 21 regular humans on staff," my father replies, sounding like he's getting annoyed.

"Don't you mean 20? Didn't one of your guards just get killed?"

"Yes, Thomas. It's a tremendous shame. He was a good man. And if you want to be technical, there are only 19 regulars here at the moment. One of my drivers just took your friend Mackenzie to the airport. Is there a point to this?"

"The *point* is that this place was just attacked. It isn't safe here anymore. Not for you, or Lyn, or me, or anyone. If four people with explosives knew where to go, you can bet there are others. Even if you arm everybody here with guns, it'll just turn this place into a war zone. You'd need your men loaded up and alert, standing every 20 meters on the top of your perimeter wall, and they'd need to be up there 24/7."

No one has even noticed me in the room, so I speak loudly. "We know who sent those people. We can always take the fight back to him."

My father steeples his fingers, thinking. "I'm sure you mean Torden, and for sure, we have had our differences for many years. But to send people on a suicide mission, strapped with explosives? That would be a radical move, even for him. Besides, we're not the ones trying to punish him. We're the Prime Order. I would think he'd try to take out leaders of the High Order instead, though of course Kevin is one, and that thought gives me no more comfort. The more likely scenario is that this is a beginning — that perhaps any of us, of either order, could be a target."

"Those people at the gate were regulars. The High Order avoids exposure to regulars, so that makes me think this is related to the Prime Order —"

"Or no order at all," my mother says.

"Sure," I nod. "But how'd they find this place?"

My father sighs deeply. "Sadly, I should have known it was a bad idea to have Kevin appear at our gates. I can only assume you all were followed."

We led those people here. And *we* came here because I wanted to, because I was obsessed with the need to find my parents. Now, all those people are dead. Guilt settles over me like a shroud, but I force myself to shove it aside. We need to figure out what to do next. "If Torden didn't do it, then who did?"

"At the moment," my father says, "I have no idea. As you know, we lead the Prime Order, and I would see no reason for infighting. Still, I feel it's necessary for us to gather all the leaders on a call. If we're at risk, they may be, too. And I will send a message to Kevin, so he's ready, and can inform his people how he chooses."

———

TWO HOURS LATER, it's nearly midnight, but everyone in the compound seems to be awake. Outside, a crew is working to shore up the hole where the gate used to be. The old gate is mangled beyond repair. As they work, a number of others stand guard with those large, ominously foreboding rifles slung over their shoulders.

Not surprisingly, Pers and I aren't invited to my parents' call with the other leaders of the Prime Order, but when they return to the posh room that I feel silly calling *le petit salon*, we're waiting. Both have dark expressions on their faces. "What happened? What did they say?"

My father waves one hand. "It isn't what they said — the others are all fine and, so far, have seen no suspicious activity, though now of course they will each be on high alert."

"Then what's the issue?"

"Orkan. He didn't join the call. In fact, when we reached out to others in Paris, they said he was nowhere to be found."

"That doesn't sound good."

"No, no it doesn't."

"So what?" Pers asks. "Do you think he's turned on you guys or something?"

"We have known Orkan Zidane for a very long time. I would find it extremely hard to think there is a rift between us, or that he would choose to attack even if he had the most grave concerns. The Prime Order discusses our problems. We work things out."

"Okay, if it's not that, if he's not behind the attack, then who is? And where is he?"

"We fear," my mother begins, "based on what happened here today, that Orkan may be in trouble. He may even have been... killed." Her throat catches as she speaks the last word, and I realize this is a friend they're talking about. I tore apart Paris when I thought Zee was dead. I have an idea how they must feel, and now I know what I need to do.

21

UNDER THE STARS

I can't sleep, mostly due to the fact that every time I close my eyes, I see the attack, the explosions, all over again. I figure true rest is out of the question for the night, so I wander the upper floors of the mansion where there are endless hallways lined with doors. They're probably living quarters for all the people staying here, so I avoid opening any of the doors at random. Proving me correct, one on my left swings open, sending a widening beam of light into the dark hall, and a man who looks to be in his forties steps out wearing pajamas. He places the remains of his dinner tray on the floor to one side, like this is some swanky hotel and he just finished with his room service. Which seems like exactly what he did.

Not wanting to wake anyone else, I use EM communication to say a single word: "Sorry." Then I slip past him, continuing to haunt the long, dim halls.

Once things become monotonous, I take the stairs down to the main floor, figuring I'll go outside and walk the grounds, though definitely not near the front gate. I've had enough of that for one night.

To one side, behind my parents' chateau, there's a long, low building that appears to have been stables, but at some point was converted into a multi-car garage for my parents' drivers and their sleek black sedans. I walk past it, counting the bays. Seven, eight...

"I know what you're doing, Lyn," someone says from somewhere nearby. In the millisecond between hearing it and recognizing the voice as Percival, I gasp and jump. After the insanity of the night, having someone appearing out of the darkness scared the shit out of me. My bad.

Suddenly I see him as a halo of light blue comes to life around him. He's leaning against the outside of the long garage, one leg bent to place the sole of that foot against the wall, and I watch the puffy steam of his breath billow out and dissipate in the cool night air. He looks cool and relaxed, the exact opposite of how I feel. *But if he's relaxed, why the blue glow...?* Looking down, I see tiny arcs of electricity jumping between my fingers, and immediately douse my power. Maybe he was just mimicking me. "You know what I'm doing? What does that mean?"

Percival barks a single quick laugh at my reaction as he pushes off the wall and walks gently across the gravel path to stand before me. "Orkan is missing in Paris. Torden was last doing his dirty work in Paris. You hate Torden — for good reason, of course. So, anyway, add all that up, and I know what you're doing. Are you leaving now? Is that why you've come to the garage? Did you line up a ride to the airport or something? Did you even tell your parents you were going?"

"No. I mean, yes. And no," I say, then grunt in annoyance. "Yes, I'm going to Paris to hunt down Torden, and hopefully find Orkan alive. No, I haven't told my parents. Yet. And no, I'm not here for a ride. I'll go in the morning. I'm just here because I can't sleep."

Percival reaches out and takes both of my arms in his hands, a gesture so familiar. "I wasn't there today, not until it was over. It must have been horrible."

"That's an understatement." Had I zapped people to death with electricity before? Yes. Had I seen their entire bodies explode? Definitely not. And I can tell you, there is a significant difference in terms of mental trauma, especially when one was self-defense and the other was just senselessness.

We start to walk in the darkness, under trees, just to have something to do. For a long while, we don't say anything, and after a few minutes, he reaches out for my hand. I don't pull away, entwining my fingers in his. It feels good. We see a small gazebo tucked amid the slanting shadows of the grove, and he guides me there, toward a bench within.

As we sit, Pers pulls me in for a hug and I let that happen, too. *God, I've missed this. Missed him.* I wrap my arms around his waist and bury my face against his chest. "I'm so sorry about what I did to you and Zee when we were little. I don't even remember doing it."

"And I don't remember it happening. But hey, if you never made me an EM, I'd probably never have traveled to Paris or Geneva, or, you know, had quite as many wild adventures." He laughs again, this time with warmth.

"I mean it. I really did you two wrong. I can't fix it, or — wait!" I look up at him with a strange hope. "I'm with my parents *here*. Maybe I can fix it! Maybe *here*, with them nearby, I can undo what I did!"

"No," he says calmly but firmly, pulling me tighter to him. "No, I don't want you to do that."

"But... why? I totally altered your life."

"You *have* totally altered my life. In more ways than one. And the most important one is this: I know that EMs tend to *be with* other EMs. If you turn me back into a regular, that would sort of mess up my long-term plans."

I peer up into his eyes as they glint in the silver-blue moonlight. I don't want to ask the question, but I have to. "Which are... what?"

"To spend as much of my life as you'll let me with you."

Desperately, I lean forward and kiss him, needing to do it so, so much. From all the fear and pain and death and danger, but also from a true recognition that this is what I really want. Now that I hear him say it so plainly, I understand. I *really* want to be with Percival. I weave my hands into his shaggy blond hair and pull him in to keep kissing me. *Don't stop.*

And we don't, sliding gently to the floor of the gazebo, surrounded by its low wall, in the early hours of morning, stars twinkling in the blackened sky, and us out of sight from the world. He helps me out of my jacket, and I unbutton his shirt. Then he pulls my t-shirt up and away, and soon we're skin on skin, two as one in the cold night air. I lie back full of ready excitement, but the icy wood floor below me causes me to gasp and tense. Percival pauses, unsure. *No, no, don't stop,* I think, and as if he reads my mind, he gently slides my jacket under my shoulders. After that, his warmth is more than enough to shield me from the cold. *Don't stop,* I think again, eyes focused on his. Then I say those same words aloud and we dive into the pleasures of each other.

Thankful to have my friend back, my lover back, I realize one thing clearly: however it began, our love has been growing for years. I love him and I don't want to be without him again, no matter what mistakes we might make along the way. And then, all conscious thought is lost to a wave of unbridled joy.

22

AFTERGLOW

Once our bodies start to cool down after the exertion, the night air bites at me much more than it had just minutes before, so we shuffle on our clothes. But neither of us wants to leave this spot, not yet. We sit back on the bench, arm in arm.

I don't want to break the spell, but an idea forms that won't leave me alone. "I don't understand it, you know? What they're talking about, me using *them* to do crazy things. I don't even know what it's like, even if I did manage to change you."

Pers rubs my shoulder. "Try now. Your parents are not that far away. Try now to tap into it and tell me what it's like."

I hesitate, but I feel like I have to do it. If I leave for Paris in the morning, I might never get another chance. I fill myself with electro-magic, glowing faintly blue in the darkness. Percival does the same, and though we've received a charge at the same time, and used power together, we've never just *sat around* full of power together. I know I can tap into his well, and he can do the same to me, so instinctively, I feel for him with my power. It feels familiar, just as his warmth next to me does.

Next, I reach out toward the chateau, across the tree lined

grounds. I don't know how this works, and maybe I'm too far away, but no, something's there. "I think I can sense them, but it's hard to explain. Sort of like a tinkling wind chime in the distance. No, two." Suddenly, I realize I've heard it before, not just the whole day we've been here, but all the time spent with Torden, too. "I have felt it before, many times. But it's so faint, it's easy to ignore, like a mild ringing in the ears."

Beside me, I feel Percival exploring with his electromagic, but it seems haphazard, unable to find the source of the sound I hear.

And that makes me sad, so sad. I love him, and I made him like this, but I was a child and I made him like a child's version of the real thing. What was it Torden had said when he had us trapped in Paris? He said Percival was lower on the power scale than the rest of us. Timidly, I decide to bring that up, knowing the words upset him at the time. "Pers, you know when Torden told us about his stupid EEMS levels?"

"Yeah, how could I forget," he says. "Everyone's higher than me."

"No, no, that's not true. I mean, he said you were average —"

"I believe the words he used were *a five or possibly a four*. Out of ten. And he said I *fail to impress him*."

Feeling with EM power, I know it to be true. I can see the deficiencies in his ability to use electromagic. "But even with that, you're in the middle. There are others who are lower, much lower."

"I guess," he says, and though it isn't like he's wailing and crying with pain, I can tell it bothers him, at least a little.

I reach into his well and my body glows brighter.

"Hey! You're gonna have everyone rushing outside to see what's going on, Lyn."

"*Shhh!*" I say harshly, closing my eyes. "Give me a second, okay?"

Like a child's version...

Like a child...

My eyes pop open. "Oh my God."

Pers pulls back in concern. "What? What is it?"

"I — I don't even know how to say it. How to ask."

"Ask what? Come on, you can ask me anything. You know you

can." He bobs his head, urging me to go ahead, and I am so scared, knowing that I made a huge mistake by changing his life when I was a little, self-centered kid.

But I did it because I wanted to be with him more. And I still do.

"If this idea is stupid or insane or insulting, just say no, and we'll never talk about it again, okay?"

Pers chuckles. "Sure, fine. You're not going to offend me. Just ask your question."

Once more I reach into his well, to be sure. I have to be sure, because if I ask and then I fail, I know he'll never forgive me, and there will always be something in his eyes when I look at him. I couldn't bear that.

But I feel sure. Really, really sure.

"What would you say if I told you that I can... I don't know... *finish* the job, so to speak? Fix the thing I did to you when I was a little kid and had no idea what I was doing?"

He blinks and grins. "I have no idea what you mean by that, but tell me more."

I steel myself, then ask in a quiet voice. "What would you say if I could make you as strong with electromagic as I am?"

Percival's eyes go wide, almost bugging out. "No way."

I smile broadly. "Yes, I really think I can."

"You're shitting me. Don't make fun of me, okay."

This time I'm the one grabbing his arms. "I am *not* shitting you. I really think I can do this. Right now, I can feel the well of your power, compare that to mine, and feel the strength of my parents nearby. I got this."

Pers looks genuinely excited. Giddy, almost. Then his smile fades. "What's the downside?"

"Huh?"

"I mean, what happens if you can't? Does it kill me? Burn electromagic out of me? Give me cancer, or migraines for life, and anything bad like that? There's always a downside."

I think about it. He's right. What *is* the downside? For a third time, I feel the well of his power, and the things I would have to do to make that change, almost like pounding the wall of a building to see how steady it is. "None of those things. Just this: if I fail, you'll be exactly as you are today, no change. And that will mean absolutely nothing to me because I love you." The millisecond those words are out of my mouth, I realize it's the first time I've said it *for real*.

"You do?"

I'm ready for this. I am. *I am.* "Yes. I do. I love you. Whether you're a EEMS 1 or an EEMS 10. I don't care about Quotient or Torden's scale, I just care about you."

"I love you, too," he says, leaning down for a passionate, joyful kiss. "But please, never mention Torden's dumbass EEMS scale again." And he laughs, and I'm so glad. "Let's give it a try."

Nodding, I can't take the smile off my face. I'm in love, not just in my head, but out loud. It makes it real. And now, I have a chance to take a random act of selfishness from my past and maybe do something to make it better.

I close my eyes again, still grinning, until I realize all the exuberance is hurting my concentration. I force myself to put on a neutral expression and reach out with EM power, in two directions — to the chateau and my parents, and into Percival's well.

At first, it's slow, like I want to build a great cathedral when I've never set a single stone before or nailed a single board. But as I start to make progress, it goes quicker and quicker, and the smile returns to my face. Percival's well of electromagic power grows and expands until I can't do any more. It feels like I'm standing on tiptoes in my mind, trying to elevate as much as possible, but knowing I've reached my limit.

Slowly, I let my EM power fade, and along with it the blue glow surrounding me dims to nothing.

At the same time, I feel Percival come alive with power, his brilliance of blue making the gazebo shine like a tiny sun from within. He's grinning and laughing, looking at himself like he's brand new.

"What is going on out here?" I hear a man shout. My father. *Shit.* I'm sure the two of us going off like disco balls on steroids got his attention.

Pers douses his electromagic as Dad steps up into the gazebo. He's staring, not at me, but at Percival, as if he's looking at an alien from outer space. He squints and starts to glow faintly with power, clearly sensing something changed and trying to find out what.

Finally, my father turns to me. "You did this to him? Just now?"

I nod.

"*Incredible.*"

23

AN ARRIVAL

In the morning, I'm in my room alone, but the nearly constant staccato of footfalls in the hall makes it clear something is happening. I quickly get dressed.

In the hall, everyone is moving. Not running. Not in fear, but with some kind of mutual interest toward the front of the chateau. I slide into the flow and go with them, bumping into Percival almost immediately. "What's going on?"

"No idea," he says.

A woman about my age overhears us and interjects, her words heavily accented, but she isn't French. Immediately, I'm reminded of Signore Bernasconi's voice. *She must be Italian.* Switzerland is basically a crossroads, and an EM fortress in the middle of it all is bound to draw people like us from all over Central Europe. "Someone has come. From Paris. A woman who was with the Prime Order there." Without another glance, she slips past a few of the others as we all make our way outside.

There, in the middle of the gravel driveway, is a grey-haired woman surrounded by four of my parents' armed guards. "Is this all necessary?" the woman asks, nodding toward the guns. "I would prefer a cup of tea. And perhaps a shower." She doesn't look like a threat to me, she just looks tired.

My mother appears, stepping forward. "Put the guns down. This is a friend of mine." She walks up to the new arrival and wraps her arms around the woman in a warm embrace. And that makes me realize that my own mother didn't even greet *me* that way. I'm suddenly... feeling something. Jealousy? No, of course not. Don't be ridiculous. "It's good to see you, Lauren, but what brings you to us? As you can see, recent events have us all a little jumpy."

"A feeling I share," Lauren says. Her eyes scan the crowd that has formed. "Paris has been compromised, and Orkan is missing." All around me, people gasp and begin muttering to each other with concern.

"Missing? Or taken?" My father says as he makes his way through the crowd toward Mom and Lauren.

"Taken, most likely," she says.

My father nods. "Then we have to assume that he was forced to reveal our location. That explains our recent visitors." Lauren asks what this means, and briefly Dad explains, gesturing toward the crudely repaired gate. "Do you have any idea who would attack you in Paris, and us here? Is it Torden Detonde?"

Lauren twists her face in a grimace. "I can only tell you what I saw. People arrived, a large group. Then, chaos. Explosions. Everyone ran in the commotion, but I doused my power and hid. They didn't find me, but I could hear what they were doing. They beat Orkan until he was taken away, then they freed Anton and Agnès Bisset from their cell."

My father scratches at his chin, thinking. "If they were brazen enough to attack you in the middle of Paris and found out our location so that they could send others here on a suicide mission, then I fear our old friend Orkan may be in great danger. If he isn't already dead."

"If the Bissets are part of it, you can guarantee that Torden is, too," I say.

"Yes, it would seem likely. Apparently, he has decided to move on."

"What does that mean?" I ask.

My father fixes me with a steely, hard look. "For many years we have disagreed, sometimes bitterly. But it was always a clash of *ideas*, not of arms. If Torden is now willing to kill Prime Order leaders like Orkan or myself, he has changed things greatly. I suspect this means all-out war."

Percival chimes in beside me. "He's going to expose EMs to the world."

Shaking his head, Dad sighs. "Yes, and more. This is a coup attempt, and if it succeeds, Torden will have an army at his disposal. Not only will regular people discover the truth of electromagicians, they'll likely be collateral damage in a battle that may change the direction of human history."

"We need to stop him," I say. "I'm going to Paris in the morning."

"He may not be there, or at least not anymore," my mother says, worry clear on her face. And that's when I realize that, welcoming hug or not, it hasn't even been a full day since I got here. Twenty years apart. Twenty hours together. I tell myself that I'll come back, but who knows? Maybe I won't live long enough for a *second* second chance.

"Marianne," my father says solemnly, turning toward my mother. "You know what we have to do."

She nods, and I will never know what they meant with that exchange.

Because that's when the bullets start to fly.

24

A MOMENT FROM A DREAM

A large covered truck — not a van, but instead something that looks military surplus — skids to a halt just outside the half-broken gate, and three men in protective gear jump out.

They don't wait for words or gestures, they just start shooting. I see a flash of red that is now all-too-familiar on my left as some EM I don't know goes down. I hear the odd dry clacks of metal hitting plaster, see the particles rain down from the impact. I don't have time to think, I just grab for Percival, turn our backs to the shooters, and pull him down to crouch with me on the gravel drive. It's foolish — we're still wide open and in mortal danger.

Something whizzes past my head and… ricochets off in another direction. I realize there's a glow around us, not the light blue glow my skin takes on when I'm full of EM power, but something like a half-dome of energy hovering over Pers, me, and a couple of the others nearest to us. I have no idea what it is, but I know it's coming from me.

Percival grabs my hand, looking at the shell around us in amazement. "How are you doing that?" he says, and you know, what the hell am I going to say in response? I don't have a clue. "Electromagnetic force field? That's a new one. Can you make it bigger?"

"I— I don't know how I made it like this. But I can try." I push outward with my EM power, and sure enough, the shell surrounding us grows in size. Others see what's happening and dive inside for protection.

Carefully, slowly, Percival tests standing up and finds that he just fits inside the protected space. He flinches as a volley of bullets bounce off the glowing surface terrifyingly close to his head. "Time to end this," he says, and he fires thick bolts of energy from both hands. Though I keep my attention on maintaining the shell, I'm still able to spin around and watch. Percival's electricity easily passes through my force field — I guess because they're made of the same thing — and rakes across the men shooting at us from the pseudo-military vehicle outside the gate. Those men convulse, involuntarily firing their weapons in all directions before collapsing, dead. But Pers continues, maybe because none of us have any idea if more gunmen are waiting to hop out at any moment. He fires both of his bolts into the body of the vehicle. At first nothing happens. Then, other EMs around us join in, and soon there are a dozen streams of energy hitting the truck in many places. One of them must land on something critical, perhaps sparking a gas line or the tank itself, because a moment later, the truck is lifted off the ground in a fiery explosion. The concussive force of the blast knocks all of us backward and knocks the wind out of me.

As I catch my breath, I realize my force field is gone. I glance past Percival, spinning to look back toward the street in fear, expecting to see the barrel of some gun pointed directly at my head. But there's no human movement, not anymore. There are just flames and smoke, and a truck that looks like it will soon be nothing but a metal shell.

Around me, people — EMs and regulars — are hurt, bleeding, dying, and dead. "Mom and Dad!" I shout, but my only answer is groans and labored breathing. *Where are they?* Pers follows me as I step gently through the scattered group of victims.

And then I see her. My mother, face down in the gravel, six or seven wet red blotches dotting the back of her sweater and dress. I run. "Mom!" I slide to a stop in the gravel beside her, hand to her shoulder, not knowing what to do. But I can feel her body moving and hear her thick, wheezing intake of air. Gently, I roll her over and my heart is shattered in a thousand pieces.

She's already too pale, the blood that should be flushing her cheeks now spilling onto the ground, clotting in the dust, coating the small stones. Her eyes are only partially open and though she moves her mouth, I can only hear a horrible, gurgling sound.

I touch the fingers of my hand to her ashen cheek. "No, you don't have to say anything. I— I want... No, I *need* to apologize to you. For showing up here angry after so many years. I searched *everywhere* to find you. Not just in Geneva, but for twenty years. I know now that's what I was doing. What I've always been doing, wandering on my own... always on my own. Too quick to push others away. Because I wasn't looking for *them*. I was looking for *you*."

"L... Lyn," she manages. "Don't blame yourself. I've always... regretted what we did. I know I'm... dying. Now... I just want you to know that if I get a second chance... if that's what happens after we die... I would never leave you again... I'm so... sorry... and... I love you." Her face loses expression and goes slack, and I know all too well what that means.

I shout and wail and pull her close to me, but there are no words, just sound. Thick, harsh sobs and inhuman noise coming from my throat because my mother is dead.

My mother is dead.

My mother is dead.

———

I SIT with her body for I don't know how long until finally a hand touches my shoulder. Slowly, I turn and find Percival crouched beside me, his shirt stained with blood. Is he hurt? No, he was with me, and somehow I protected him, and others. This blood... must be from others. Maybe he was helping the injured. Maybe he was tending to the dead.

Dead.

I try to speak, but I've ripped up my throat from screaming and crying. I swallow, hard, trying to make it possible to ask the one question I need to ask. "My father—?"

Percival solemnly shakes his head, and I shudder with new sobs.

Twenty years apart. Twenty hours together. And now, they are both truly gone.

I would say my heart breaks again, but suddenly I feel hollow. I have no heart.

I have only the gaping sorrow of emptiness inside me, a hole I know cannot be refilled, not by time, by anything, or by anyone else.

I only feel empty.

No, that's not true.

There is one thing more than this horrible hole inside me. One thing that slowly allows me to lower my mother's dead body to the ground and push myself up to stand.

Though wetness has left streaks down my cheeks, tracks through blood and grime, my tears stop their flow. My jaw sets.

Because the one thing I have left inside is a promise.

A promise of revenge.

PART III

A TURN FROM THE SUN

25

AM I SO BLIND I CANNOT SEE?

We stand outside Paris-Orly staring at the bustle of the world like we have no idea what the hell to do next.

Because we don't.

Also, because, personally, I've never landed at Orly before, only Charles de Gaulle, the larger airport north of the city. Look at me, sounding like a freaking expert on Paris travel. Would you like to know where to get the best croissants? How the hell would I know? I spent all my time here tracking some wacko — Torden, of course — trying to make EM babies and steal EM power with a damned underground machine.

"What now?" Percival asks. When we left the plane, he politely offered to carry my duffle bag as well as his overnighter, but boyfriend or not, I can fend for myself. I drop my bag to the cement walkway and scan the signs.

Yeah, they're written in both French and English, but *Taxi* means *Taxi*. I figure, we'll, screw comfort and let's get this over with; I don't want to be in Paris long enough to worry about a place to stay, despite the fact that the sun is setting and if we don't get a hotel, I imagine we'll be sleeping on airport benches. Still, I'm too mad to worry about logistics. We're going to the

Bissets' house directly. If they're there, we kill them or incapacitate them or whatever, and free Orkan — if he's still alive. Wait. Maybe first we torture them to tell us where Torden is. And then we head back to the airport and fly home. Well, not this airport. I think we need to go to CDG to fly to NYC. But what do I know? Paris travel expert, I am not. And, damn it, I'm rambling. Lack of sleep.

"This way," I say, picking up my duffle again and following the arrows for Taxi.

Percival rushes to catch up. "So, what? Go to the Bissets' house? Do you even remember the address?"

I pause, thinking. I don't remember the address, but I remember a lot of other things about where they lived. *Above a section of the catacombs, though that might mean half the city. Across from a park. What was that park's name?* "Do you remember the park across from their house? What was that called?"

"Uh," Percival says, biting his bottom lip in a way that looks thoughtful and dumb and really cute all at the same time. "No, sorry. But — I remember it had a fence around it. And there was a big road on the south end. And it was pointy at the corners. Plus, it was near that cafe!"

I bob my head left and right dramatically, sarcastically. "We'll just tell the cab driver that, then, I guess."

Pers scoffs. "What? There's no way someone's gonna know where to take us based on just that!"

I stare at him. You know, *that* stare.

"Oh. Ha. Very funny. Well, it's not like you have any better idea."

But I think I do. I remember the park was south of the Seine — the Left Bank, as they call it. Amazing what trivial stuff sticks in your head. And it was beside a large road, just like Percival says. And one other thing... "There was a sort of lake or pond in it, too." I dig out my phone, glad that I paid for service in Geneva that *also* works in Paris. I pop open the map app, and swipe back and forth, scanning the south side of Paris for a park — pointy corners, with a lake or pond — whose name I can't recall. But I think it'll come back to me once I see it, and it does. "There! *Parc Montsouris*. The house was just to one side..."

Percival is looking at his own phone, attempting the same visual recognition as me. He swipes again, answering me in a distant voice. "No, that name doesn't sound familiar..." I punch him in the arm. "Ow! What's your problem?"

"The name *is* familiar, because it's *right*. I switch over to street view, dropping the marker along the west side of the park, and there, plain as day, is the Bissets' house. The only thing it's missing are the temporary barricades from the power company that were there to hide access to the catacombs. I turn the screen toward Pers.

"Oh. Oh yeah. That's totally it." He smiles.

I roll my eyes, but can't hide a smile of my own. Percival can be an idiot, but I suppose he's *my* lovable idiot. "Come on," I say, fast-walking in the direction of the taxi stand.

———

THE BISSETS' house looks the same as before, and they've somehow even managed to keep the power company barricades up as well, which startles me. At least until I realize that their transgressions in the catacombs were EM business, and that no regular police officer was after them or even aware they'd done anything. How they turned the tables on the Prime Order, though, I have no idea.

It's dark now, which I hope will help us, because obviously we aren't walking up and knocking on the front door. Scanning the area, I see no one else around, so we seize the opportunity and power ourselves up, just enough to float over the lowest part of the structure and down into the Bissets' garden.

Silence. Darkness. No movement.

Well, shit, they're old. Maybe they're in bed. I tap my phone and find out it's 10:14pm. If we sneak up on the Bissets' sleeping at 10:14pm, I am going to be sorely disappointed in their old asses. All this makes me realize that I *want* the fight. I want them to know we're coming. I pretend to stumble and knock over one of the chairs on the patio, making a series of loud metal-on-stone clangs that ring out in the night.

"Lyn!" Percival whispers. "Jesus, could you be more careful?"

I look away, knowing that even in the dim light, he would see it in my eyes. See my intentions.

Still, the house remains as it was. I walk to the back door and jiggle the handle, surprised to find it open easily. I guess the fact that the Bissets' patio is enclosed on all sides by steep, thick walls makes them confident enough to leave the garden door unlocked.

We search the house, full of its old trinkets, memories that anywhere else might look like fond reminders. In this place, it just makes me angrier, knowing the awful things this couple is capable of, and wanting their long miserable lives simply to end. But no one is home.

"What now?" Pers asks once again. I try not to be irritated by the question.

"We check other places. Catacombs, Orkan's building, and beneath that church, where we found them before."

It takes hours, but we do. Each one. And we find nothing and no one.

———

At least an hour after midnight, having no better ideas, we return to the Bissets' dark and empty house. "We should get a hotel room, try again in the morning," Percival says.

"Hold on, I have a thought." Sure, it's late, but we need answers now. I pull out my phone, then scroll through my contacts and find Nurse Charlotte Laffitte. I almost call her number, but figure I'll try texting first.

Do you know where Anton Bisset is? Urgent.

I don't expect an answer right away, but still, I get one just a few moments later.

Bisset has been on holiday for several days.

What day is it? Or is Nurse Laffitte just a night owl? I realize suddenly that she's a *nurse*. For all I know, she could be at work. I write back, quickly. *Where?*

I have no idea.

Another dead end.

"What was all that?" Pers asks.

"That nurse, the one who first introduced us to Anton Bisset. She says he's *on holiday*. No idea where." *On holiday* is perhaps the most European phrase of all time.

"Shit," he says. Then Percival starts to wander around the Bissets' living room aimlessly.

I fume. I hate this feeling of uselessness. Of wasting time. My parents died because the Bissets are up to something very bad — and I know it involves Torden Detonde, who I myself am responsible for freeing on the world. I *have* to find them as quickly as I can. I try to tell myself that it's partly to rescue Orkan, but honestly, given the explosives and guns they used at my parents' chateau, I doubt he's even alive anymore.

I'm pacing the floor when Percival speaks. "Look at this."

I grunt a response. "Come on, focus. We need to figure out where they are."

"Lyn," he says. "I think I just did."

I whirl around and see him simply staring at the wall. "What are you talking about?"

"Look at these pictures." He points at framed photos on the living room wall, three in total. "They're all taken in the same place, a house in the woods, near a lake, but the Bissets are much different ages in each one."

I walk up behind him, still angry, not trusting his judgment. Which is a mistake, because the second I actually look at the photos, I realize he's onto something. "Holy shit, they have a vacation house."

"Right," Pers says. "And you just told me the hospital thinks he on vacation."

"On *holiday*," I say, correcting him with a sarcastic laugh.

Percival shrugs. "Whatever. We just need to figure out where this place is."

Immediately, I'm moving. "Tear everything apart. Find anything you can — a utility bill, a grocery receipt from outside Paris, whatever!"

We do, but soon that same bitterness seeps in. Even having three photographs of where we think the Bissets are hiding, we have no idea where it actually *is*. "Shit!" I say, because sometimes that's all you can say.

"We could call your brother," Pers says, and I'm suddenly so, so sorry.

I can't believe what I've done.

No.

I can't believe what I've forgotten to do.

"Call my brother," I echo. "Yeah." My voice is raspy before I even start to dial. *I'm such an idiot*, I think.

Two rings and Kevin picks up. "Lyn?"

"Yeah, hey, it's me. Um, I need to tell you a couple of things. Well, I mean, I need to ask for your help, and —"

"What do you need?" I hear him tapping on a keyboard, and I make the probably unwise decision of talking about the least important thing first. Scratch that, this decision is *definitely* unwise.

"I need you to look at the Bissets' utility bills again. See if you can find any for an address that *isn't* in Paris, or at least isn't the place in the city you sent us too before. A place in the woods, on a lake."

"Okay, but where *are* you?"

I wrinkle my face and consider the irony. "We — Pers and I — are in the Bissets' house in Paris."

Tapping continues, now faster. "With them?"

"No, of course not. I just need to tell —"

"Oh, wait, I think I've got something here! A whole slew of charges at another address." Kevin says. "Let me look it up on a map." More tapping. "Heh. It's not a lake house, technically, it's a river house. It's on the Seine, southeast of the city."

"Can you text me the address?"

"Of course, but what's this all about? Aren't the Bissets in Prime

Order custody? And why aren't you with Mom and Dad in Switzerland?"

I pause, gulping hard for air. My lungs suddenly seem to have forgotten how to work, and I have absolutely no idea what word to use in all the English language to begin. "I — I —"

"Lyn?" Kevin says, now concerned. "What's going on?"

"Mom and Dad are dead," I say in a rush, not knowing any way to make the truth any less horrible and painful than it actually is.

There's a sound over the line like someone punched the air out of Kevin's chest. "What are you talking about? I just saw them. *We* just saw them, together. A day ago. You're not making any sense."

I can't help but cry, and that stops Kevin from talking. "Kev, some people showed up, first with explosives. Those were stopped before they could reach the house. But then another group showed up, and we all happened to be in the front of the chateau, on the drive. When they opened fire, we were all just *standing* there..."

"No," he says, his voice no longer the confident older brother. Now he sounds young, innocent, and terrified. "*No.*"

"I'm sorry, it's true. A bunch of the people were killed. Including Mom and Dad. I'm... sorry."

Kevin's voice shifts, now sounding almost angry. "When did this happen? You said you were in Paris, right? *When did this happen?*"

I think. The whole thing, ever since we went to see my parents, has been insanely whirlwind. "About 24 hours ago." Even I can't believe how much has changed so quickly.

"A day," he says, in a daze. "They were killed a *day* ago, and you call me up with questions about a river house first? What the hell is wrong with you, Lyn?" He breaks down, sobbing, and though we've been at odds over the years, he's still my brother, and I wish I could be there with him. I wish.

"I'm sorry, really. I should have called you right away. I — I just —"

"Just what? Just thought about *yourself?*"

He's right. I was only thinking about myself, and I've done that for too long. But I want to be different now. I do. "I'm really sorry, Kevin. I want to do better. By you, by them, by everyone. Not calling you was selfish, but it was because I was stuck inside my own head, and frankly, I was — I *am* — bent on revenge. I — I guess I wanted to act rather than think, and acting took me here, to Paris. Orkan is missing, maybe dead too, and I thought if I could get to Paris, find the Bissets, find Orkan if I can, then maybe I could do something to get revenge on whoever is responsible for our parents' deaths. I think it's Torden, of course, with the Bissets helping, so I wanted to follow that lead while it was still hot. I'm sorry for not calling you right away. I really am."

Maybe he believes me, or maybe he doesn't. Still, my brother clears his throat, and a semblance of the normal Kevin returns. "Yeah. Okay. I can't even believe this is true, but I guess I kept you in the dark about where they were for years. You only kept me in the dark for a day."

"Why don't we just call it even?" The second these words escape my lips, I wish I could pull them back, but, you know, that's kind of impossible.

"In a way, we are," Kevin says, much more forgiving and kind than I deserve. Until he completes the thought. "Now, neither of us will ever see them again."

26

FROM HELL'S HEART

The first four taxi drivers we talk to don't understand English, or pretend not to understand English, or straight up don't want to drive the 28 kilometers outside the city where we need to go. Luckily, the fifth shrugs and gestures for us to get in.

The slowest part of the journey, of course, is the congestion in the city. Once we're outside that, the drive is monotonous and long, to the point that I almost fall asleep. And by *almost* I mean *definitely*.

"Stop here!" Percival suddenly shouts from the back seat, and the startled driver obliges, stomping on the brakes so hard that I lurch fully awake, thinking I'm about to be launched through the front windshield.

"What the —!" I stammer.

"Sorry," Pers says to me in a whisper. "But we don't want to drive right up to the front door." He turns to the driver. "Anywhere here is good. Thanks."

The driver pulls over and says something in French that I realize is what we owe him. He also points to the digital numbers on the meter. Thankfully, I have cash from when I was traveling in secret with Torden — a period of time that already seems like it's from another life. Given the fact that I'm able to pull out a wad of crumpled euros from my pocket, it wasn't really long ago at all.

"Do you need me to wait 'ere?" the driver asks, much better at a British-tinged English than I would be butchering French.

I almost say yes, since I have no better answer for how we're going to get back to the city, but then I remember we're here to do some shit that would be really, really hard to explain, so I just shake my head and thank him for the offer. "*Non merci.* No thanks." *I just did that two languages thing again.* I grumble at myself silently.

We watch the taxi do a slow U-turn on the two-lane road, and we don't budge until the driver crests a hill and is out of sight. "Which way?" I ask once we're alone.

Percival checks his phone. "It's over there. The second driveway," he says. "But we need to plan this out. We can't just walk up. I mean, they probably will be surprised that anyone found them out here, but then again, they may be paranoid old bastards, so we need to be as sneaky as we can be."

"Also," I add. "They may not be here. I mean, good job sleuthing this place out and all, but we may be simply, you know, *wrong.*"

"We're not. We'll go through the trees, between houses. I can't tell from the satellite view if there's a fence or not, but we can just pop over it if there is. Come on."

I will say this: Mister Hospital Director and his wife must have money. I mean, I know I'm one to talk, given the wealth of my family, but the Bissets own not only a townhouse in the city, but also a riverfront cottage. A *big* riverfront cottage. We eventually come to a low brick wall that surrounds the property, zipping over it with a little bit of EM power. Percival quietly laughs as we land on the other side. "What's so funny?" I whisper.

He gestures back toward the wall. "*That.* Floating like that used to take more effort. I can really feel the difference with what you did to me. I mean, I still feel like I only understand maybe half of the way you've expanded my powers, so it'll take time. But floating felt easier."

I don't know whether that's a complaint or a compliment, so I just look away, sheepishly.

"No, it's not a bad thing. Thanks. It feels incredible to do things with ease that used to be harder."

"Um, you're welcome, I guess." I've never been very comfortable with compliments.

Pers just smiles at me, perfect teeth, a curl from his mop of hair drooping in front of one eye in a very, very distractingly attractive way. "Over there," he says, pointing to a row of thick bushes near one side of the house. "We can hide behind those and just watch for a bit. See if we can spot them, then make a plan of attack."

Thank God the bushes are there and that they are pretty dense, because the moment we reach them I spy motion inside one of windows along the side of the house. Agnès Bisset herself, the woman who took both the power and the life of our friend Hayden, is walking toward the rear of the house, in the direction of the river. She's carrying a small ceramic cup, probably coffee.

"Well, at least we know we were right about where to find them," Pers says. "Now, we just need to know how many people are here."

"Hopefully three," I say. "Anton, Agnès, and Orkan." I start to move, overconfident in my ability to knock out a couple of old timers.

"Hold on, Lyn," Pers says, gently catching me and guiding me back to a crouch. "I seriously doubt the Bissets are holding Orkan all by themselves. There will be others, most likely be armed. And if the attacks on your parents' chateau are any indication, the guards will do *anything* they have to do. We need to be ready to use some serious force."

The mere mention of my parents conjures up raw emotions. "Believe me, that won't be a problem," I say, my voice edgy and rough.

Percival gives me a concerned look, but suddenly there's more to worry about. Proving Pers right in his assumptions, a guard appears from around the far side of house and heads almost directly toward us. For a moment, I think we're busted, but the man seems calm, just doing his routine patrol. Sure enough, he has a long, dark, and no doubt deadly rifle slung over his shoulder. I stifle a gasp, but Pers gently squeezes my arm. "Don't forget — you're strong."

"I'm not strong in every way. Sometimes I don't feel strong at all."

"I trust you. And, more importantly, if we don't want to start some kind of shoot-out battle, we need to take out this guy *silently*. My guess is that he's looping the house, and that he's done it so many times, he's bored to death. And I'd guess he's going to walk right past us on the other side of this hedgerow. When he gets near, I'll zap him once, hard. Then we just need to drag him out of sight. Got it?" he says. I nod.

Amazingly, the plan works exactly as Pers outlined it. Maybe two minutes later, I'm crouched behind the bushes with a dead, electro-cuted guard, as Percival relieves the man of his gun. I should feel something about this. Something about killing this person. But these are the people — all of them — that are responsible for killing my parents. Instead of feeling guilt, I just look away. *You all brought this on yourselves.* It's a callous, almost hateful thought, and I'm not proud of it. In fact, it starts to eat at me a bit. No, it starts to *burn* me. But it does feel a lot like the truth.

"How many more?" I ask.

Pers shrugs. "Don't know, but I'd guess several more. If Orkan isn't already dead, there will be one or two to guard him. And the Bissets are ancient, so they probably have a couple of bodyguards, as well. So that's my guess. Four more guards, two Bissets. And save Orkan if possible."

"We have a wildcard," I say.

"Which is?"

"The ability to block bullets." *If I can remember how.* But I think I can, if I try hard enough. Once I learn something, it tends to stick around.

"Right, but let's say you do that, and then let's say I'm inside your protective bubble and they come out firing. Yes, I have a gun now, but I suspect that your shield works the same way from both sides. If I try to shoot from inside it, it will probably just ricochet like crazy, and that's not likely to be good for either of us."

He's right. Damn.

But then I realize how to make it work. I tell Pers and he starts grinning, ear to ear. "Let's do it."

Moments later, I'm walking out in the open, across the front lawn of the Bissets' riverfront vacation home. "Hello! Anyone home?" I shout.

Quickly, the calm and quiet are shattered as two armed men burst out the door and stand before me on the porch of the house. They're smiling. They think they know EMs are susceptible to bullets, so they take their time. I almost feel sorry for them.

Slowly, deliberately, they raise their weapons. There will be no negotiations here. I kneel, but still they prepare to fire. That tells me all I need to know. They would kill me in cold blood, so I no longer have any concern for what's about to happen.

I pulse out a shell of EM power, ready.

And they begin to fire.

Their bullets bounce off the shell, making distant whiffing sounds as they land among the trees or rip through leaves.

Then Percival appears.

No, of course, he can't fight back from within my bulletproof shield. But he can use the gun *outside* my shield and flank them while they're distracted.

It takes seconds.

The guards fall on the porch, and in seconds, silence once again returns. But it doesn't last. The sound brings more armed men. We planned for that, and Pers once more ducks behind the bushes. Two new would-be heroes fire at me, and once more, I deflect their attack. And once more, Percival drops them where they stand.

We wait, ready for a third round.

It never happens.

Finally, I stand and walk up to the porch, climbing the trio of stairs. I step over the dying, ignoring them and entering the house. Percival is just behind me. All part of the plan.

We go room to room, at first finding nothing. Finally, and pretty much how we expected, we're left with the stairs going down to a dark basement. This is it.

I take the first step down and hear a gunshot. The bullet pings away, because I'm not a total idiot and I'm ready for this, a sphere of protection surrounding me once again. Another shot fires and another, and honestly, I'm hoping for more. *Run out of ammo, you shitheads.* They do, which honestly surprises me. I hear clicks. Fricking *clicks.* Like this is some kind of ridiculous movie, and their next idea will be to throw their weapon at me in futility. I continue down the stairs, still holding my protective energy field in place, with Percival behind. He's not *within* the shield, so he can still shoot, but the presence of the circle around me provides a major screen for anything that might come his way. It doesn't matter. The people in the basement no longer have anything to shoot at us, and instead they run at me with knives. Two of them. Two more pops sound from over behind me and they drop. Then Pers is done with the gun, because the only people left in the house are the Bissets cowering in a corner, and Orkan — alive still, thankfully, gagged and weary on a plain wooden chair.

Anton Bisset puffs up in some sort of seriously misguided show of bravado. "What are you going to do, shoot us, too?"

"Probably," Pers says, and I almost laugh as both Bissets stagger backward, shaken. I couldn't care less about their fragile emotions. As far as I'm concerned, these people directly murdered my parents.

I go to Orkan and start to free him from his bonds. The Bissets have no weapons that I know of, and if that leaves them with nothing but EM power, there isn't anything they can do to me, so I ignore them. Finally, I undo a knot and Orkan is free. "Are you okay?" I ask.

"Ye— yes. Thank you," he says, rubbing his wrists. "Your parents?"

I shake my head, trying to avoid crying in this particular setting. *Damn it.* Of course, the Bissets see my reaction.

"So... we succeeded. Well, they deserved what they got," Anton Bisset says. His wife just smiles a wicked, awful smile, smugly pleased with herself.

I raise my hand. But really... what am I going to do? Donate some of my EM power to them? It's pointless.

"You're pathetic," Agnès Bisset says. "This is why we need to take charge and begin the announcement of our cause. The young and foolish like yourselves are constantly running around *thinking* you're doing good, but in truth, you have no idea what you're doing at all. You children simply do not see the bigger picture. You can't seem to grasp the master plan." She's practically spitting with disgust at me.

It gives me an idea. "And what's that?" I ask.

"To finally show this ignorant world who belongs in control," Anton says.

"You?" I scoff. "You're powerless."

They both laugh. "Only to someone like yourself," Anton says. "You can use your power on us, or we on you, and it makes no difference. But on regulars..."

Percival sees me eyeing his borrowed rifle. "Think about it hard, Lyn. Killing means something," he says quietly.

"I know."

"Shoot us if you're going to, then." Agnès Bisset says with a dismissive smirk. "Get it over with."

"No," I say forcefully.

"Then you truly cannot do *anything* to us at all," Anton says. He grins.

But he's oh so very wrong.

I fill myself once more with power and reach out for them. *I did this once, in the other direction. I'm pretty sure I can do it again, just flowing in reverse. But it was so long ago. How can I —?* Still, my anger makes me try.

Anton feels it first, what I'm doing to him. "*Mon Dieu!*" he gasps. A second later, Agnès feels it, too.

But it's too late.

I reach into them, though I really have no idea what the hell I'm doing. Still, at one point as a stupid kid, I gave two regulars electromagic power, just because I was near my parents, two very strong electromagicians. Now, in the presence of Percival, an EM I made strong all on my own, I reach into the two bitterly twisted people standing before me and take that power away.

I render the Bissets useless, in seconds.

They feel it.

They *feel* it.

And I'm not happy, but I'm not sad. They deserve this pain. They deserve it.

Anton drops to his knees, howling, suddenly confronted with something he never thought he'd feel. Powerlessness. His wife doesn't even attempt to console him, because she has both hands at her chest like she can't breathe. She crumbles beside him helplessly. Together on the floor, but each lost in their personal hell, they moan and writhe.

Now, I think. *Now, if I send a bolt of energy into either of them, they won't just lap it up like a dog at a water bowl. They'll die.* But I don't.

There's no need.

I've done worse than kill the Bissets.

I've taken away their lives.

27

_____

PATHS DIVIDE

It takes forever, but we score a cab back to the city. Orkan comes with us, but he doesn't speak. He's in a daze, and I don't even have the heart to ask what he's been through. With great exertion, he manages to give us a heartfelt thanks as we drop him at Place des Vosges, the same place where we first met. Moment later, Percival and I are on the way to the airport.

Without a destination.

Shit.

"We don't even know where we're going," I say abruptly, my mood dark.

"We don't?" Pers says. "I thought we were going home."

"And then what? Just forget about what really happened? Who's really responsible?"

Percival snaps his fingers. "Your brother!"

"No, not Kevin, Torden," I say with a sigh.

Pers shakes his head with a quick laugh. "Of course it's Torden. I mean, your brother can help us find him. Phone records. Or texts or email, whatever. Kevin can hack all that shit, right?"

"I guess."

"Then call him."

A moment later, Kevin answers the phone. "Lyn. Is everything okay? What happened with the Bissets?"

"I —" I begin, not sure exactly how to respond. According to my parents, Kevin doesn't know what I can do, and maybe knowing it would put him in violation of The Oath of the High Order in some way. So I'm vague. "I took care of the Bissets. And Orkan Zidane is fine, just out of juice at the moment. Once he gets a charge, I think he'll be all right."

"What do you mean you *took care of the Bissets*? Did you kill them?"

"No!" I say, too forcefully.

"Imprison them? Break their legs? I don't understand, Lyn." Why the hell can't Kevin just move on?

Screw it, this is exhausting, I think. *They can't punish Kevin for just some words someone says to him, can they?* "I took away their EM power. They're regulars now." I say all this and immediately know I should've kept my big mouth shut.

"That's *impossible*," Kevin whispers. But somehow, strangely, he doesn't even sound like he believes himself. He must have suspected all along why our parents left me. Maybe he didn't know exactly, but he's no idiot, and he's had 20 years to think about it.

"Trust me, it's possible. I did it." Then another idea comes to me, and I realize that what I've done isn't just taking away the most important part of the Bissets. "I suppose it is a death sentence, though. If they've been doing what Torden's been doing — sucking up other people's power to prolong their lives — and they're unnaturally old, then I guess this means the end of the road for them."

"Good," Kevin says sternly. "To hell with them."

I'm stunned. My brother doesn't usually talk like that. Then I remember there's a hard side to my brother, and I don't mean just the part that never let me change the wallpaper in my room. This is the same man who took control of the New York City branch of the High Order, who was ready to use the Touchstone of Mount Hachiro to remove Torden Detonde's electromagic abilities permanently. The fact that I did it to the Bissets on my own probably just saved him time and effort. "I need another favor, though, Kev."

I know he hates when I call him *Kev*, so I expect pushback. Instead, he stuns me again. "Name it."

"I need to find Torden, to end all of this once and for all."

"And you need me to help figure out where he is. All right. Any ideas, or should I go with my best guess?"

"I'm tired of all this, and I'd really like to just know exactly. Guessing and running around the world searching for someone, well, that's something I've already done my fair share of for the past two decades or so."

"Phone records. Email records. Texts," Pers says loudly beside me, and Kevin hears it.

"Sure. And I have some other, um, *methods*. I'll call you back."

"Thanks," I say, and my brother ends the call. The taxi exits the main road with the air traffic control tower of Charles de Gaulle ahead, and for whatever reason, I realize I'm starving. I turn to Percival. "I need a coffee and some macarons."

"As you wish, m'lady" he says, donning a really atrocious English accent, grinning and bending in a bow. Percival, my knight in shining armor, just like the old stories. But honestly, if we find Torden, I might want him as my knight, riding in to save this damsel's ass. I roll my eyes and shake my head. *Stories are just stories.*

———

"Lyn," Kev says as I answer the call. It's been hours — I don't even know how many — and we've been sleeping on benches at CDG. Not just one, because I guess eventually all of their gates get used — I know, that's kinda the point of an airport — but people keep streaming in and making noise, forcing us to change places. We've moved four times. Besides, sleeping on the hard, L-shaped plastic slabs this airport considers to be furniture has literally become a pain in my neck. I'm *really* hopeful that my brother has some information that will get us out of this cycle of hell. "Two options."

I was hoping for a simpler answer. I sigh, rubbing my aching neck. "Please say Manhattan and the Bronx."

"Well, you're close on one. There were repeated calls to a cell phone in the greater New York area. I'm working to narrow that down now."

"And the other?"

"South America."

My shoulders slump. "Jesus." I was hoping for my own bed at some point soon. Yeah, the bed in the way-too-stuffy room I've had since I was a kid. All of the sudden, I'm feeling nostalgia for the damned place. And Juliet. I miss Juliet. That almost makes me choke up. Juliet has been more of a mother to me over the last 20 years than my real mother. Who is now... No. *Stop thinking about that.* "Please tell me you have something more specific than just the name of a continent."

"Of course. I worked this one out carefully, knowing we'd have to split up our efforts."

I don't like the sound of that, though I realize it's necessary. "Just tell me the nearest airport, so I can buy a ticket."

"La Chinita, Maracaibo, Venezuela. There won't be any direct flights. You could go to another airport faster, like Caracas, but it'll mean a nine-hour drive."

"No way. I'll go to the closest airport," I say. "Sleeping on an uncomfortable chair that's moving me somewhere is better than what I'm doing now."

"And if you find him?" Kevin asks.

"Same as if you find him in New York, I imagine."

"I will arrest him and use the Touchstone to take away his power," Kevin says.

"Oh, well, then we will have slightly different resolutions," I reply. Kevin doesn't respond, but I hear his breathing, heavy with anticipation. "If I find Torden in South America, I'm going to kill him."

I expect Kevin to sigh or argue, but instead he makes a sharp grunt, *mmhmm,* and I remember that it wasn't just *my* parents that were murdered. It was *ours.* "Good luck," he says. "Let's finish this."

28

INTO THE JUNGLE

I make the conscious decision not to pay attention to time, because I'm wasting so much of it flying, waiting in another airport, then flying again. The only good part, strangely, is our last layover: Panama City, Panama. An eight-hour delay due to thunderstorms in the area, and you can bet your ass that Pers and I try to leave the airport. Customs is, oddly, totally cool with us taking a romp before our next flight. Either we found the most chill agent ever, or Panama doesn't have much of a problem with smuggling or terrorism or whatever else those agents are supposed to thwart. I don't care either way, so we head out into the sunlight, excited to experience Central America for the very first time. I smile, particularly happy to inhale my first breath of non-sterile airplane or airport air in some time.

Then a wave of humidity stops me in my tracks, and immediately a bead of sweat forms on my upper lip. "Oh my God, is this *normal*?" Compared to the controlled temperatures of the airports and planes, the heat is positively oppressive. Still, everyone around us looks like it's just another day.

Percival's mouth is hanging open, and he's panting almost uncontrollably. "I'm going to need to buy new clothes," he says, waving a hand in front of his face as if that's going to cool him off at all.

One overpriced cab ride later, guided by Pers and his weather app radar, and we're in some forest park in the rain. We make our way to a remote part, trying to gain elevation with only the slightest success, and we wait. It doesn't take long. A rumbling storm blows through, full of beautiful lightning, and we charge up. I can't remember the last time, so damn it feels good.

———

EVENTUALLY, we get to Venezuela, but after how long? An eternity? It's like anything could have changed while we were either stuck in some metal and glass building on the ground, or in some metal and glass tube in the sky. Meanwhile, the Maracaibo airport is weirdly *dim*, like someone forgot to pay the electric bill or they're going for a kind of odd mood lighting. It doesn't work, given that the rest of the place is sterile concrete. Pers and I shuffle slowly through customs, generating a little bit of extra interest from the agents due to our notable lack of significant luggage, but eventually they let us go.

The airport is essentially like any other; one of those places where you just know that some percentage of the taxis — perhaps as high as 100% — are scams, but we can't tell the legitimate from the fake, so we just grab the first one that's free. Maybe the guy will overcharge us, like in Panama City, or take us on some roundabout joy ride to bump up the fare. How the hell would I know? Never been here before. The man speaks to us in what I call *Transactional English* — enough so that we can at least conduct our business. And kudos to him for that, because I speak almost zero Spanish. Whatever I learned in high school is now a jumbled mess from me trying to wade through French for months, with flecks of Italian thrown in for good measure. We ask the driver to stop and wait for us while we shop at a little roadside store for shorts and t-shirts, and the guy doesn't drive off with our pathetically minimal travel bags, so I assume he's not just a crook.

As we make our way into the city, a turn puts the sun directly in front of us, and the driver flips down his visor, exposing a photo he's taped to the back; two little girls, his kids assumedly. I feel bad for wondering if he was scamming us before. Not that being a parent inherently makes you a good person. If there's one thing I understand deeply, it's that parents can be... *complicated.*

Finally, he pulls into a wide circular drive lined with palm trees, a tall hotel standing ominously above us. It's the local outpost of some chain of fancy resorts, all arranged by my brother, Kevin, of course.

"This looks nice," Percival says. Then his examination of the entryway catches a sign that reads CASINO. "Ooh, maybe I need a white tuxedo." We step out of the taxi, once more wading into the oppressive humidity. Immediately, Pers seems to wilt. "Nah, screw that, I'm definitely not putting on a tuxedo here. I'll melt."

I turn back to pay the driver... and realize I don't have any of the local currency. Frankly, this trip was so last minute that I don't even know what the local currency is. I open my wallet and sigh. I shouldn't be surprised, based on my recent history, that the only cash I have is good only in Europe. "Hey, I'm sorry, but I forgot to get, um, Venezuelan money at the airport. Do you mind if we pay in euros?"

The driver laughs. "Mind?" he asks with a thick accent. "It is better. If you bought *bolívares* at the airport, they would be worth half of what you paid by now." I realize he's probably exaggerating, but the idea is mind-boggling. It was a 30 minute drive... Vaguely, I recall hearing that Venezuela has had a staggering rate of inflation for years; to see it in person is a little unsettling. Knowing that money isn't something that affects me too greatly, I pay and overtip. I know, I know. Rich girl privilege, to try to make me sleep better at night, feeling wonderful about my generosity. But if this guy can use the money on the two cute little kids in that photo taped to his visor, then so be it. The driver holds out a dogeared business card, gesturing for me to take it. "Please. If you need another ride while you're here, you can call me. Okay?" I nod, taking the card. Next to his phone number, his name is printed: Luis. I return the nod, though I don't say anything that locks us into some kind of long-term arrangement. *Still so paranoid.* As for Luis, he's probably in his mid-thirties, a mop of dark hair, and he gives me a warm, friendly smile as he gets back in the car and drives off.

"What now?" Pers asks.

I twist my neck in a circle, hearing several loud pops. "How long have we been traveling? And what time is it, anyway?" Traversing multiple time zones in the space of hours will always be a supremely inhuman experience.

"I haven't kept track."

"You hungry?" I ask.

Percival puts one hand on his stomach. "Nah. That airplane food is sitting like a stone."

"Me neither. So we check in and just get some sleep for now." Overhead, clouds flash with hidden lightning, though I never hear the sound of thunder. Maybe it'll rain.

Pers grins. "Seems a little crazy, being tired from sitting on our asses all day and night."

I don't disagree with what he says in concept. Our reality, however, strongly disagrees. We sleep for 10 hours.

———

OF COURSE, I wake up and the sun hasn't even risen. Damned jet lag. Percival stirs next to me, and soon we're both sitting up, wondering if it's too early to call room service for breakfast. I get out of bed and search for the menu. Kevin did put us in a resort, not a motel, after all.

I flip the pages, seeing standard tourist options. Which is to say, things that will make Americas generally feel at home. Then, near the end, there are a couple unfamiliar things. I'm kind of a "when in Rome" person, so I opt for one of those: some fried, doughnutty kinds of things called *mandocas*; I only know what they are because there's a picture next to the listing. Pers has eggs and sausage.

Our breakfast is delivered on a rolling cart a short while later by a dark-haired kid so young and innocent-looking, I wonder if he'd be old enough to work in the States. *Or maybe that just means you're getting old, Lyn Hopkins*, I tell myself. *Shut up. I'm not even 25.* Then, for some reason, I remember a time when 25-year-olds looked like senior citizens. I wonder if the delivery kid thinks that of me. I tip him with a broad smile, trying foolishly to look and act younger, maybe cooler. He thanks us and leaves, but maybe, just maybe, there was a look of confusion on his face. Or unsettled fear. But why shouldn't he be confused and afraid? Would anyone *actually* his age have a room like this at a resort? Seems unlikely.

Of the two of us, I feel like my choice was superior, because — *damn!* — *mandocas* with a little butter and a coffee are delicious.

I lean back in the chair at our oblong dining table and let myself relax, just for a moment.

"When are we gonna do what we came to do?" Pers asks in a soft voice, even though those words are nothing soft at all.

I look to my left, out the large windows of the suite Kevin arranged for us. The sun is coming up, glinting off the water to our east. It isn't the ocean — I at least had the sense to do a small amount of research on our destination while waiting on one of our connections — it's Lake Maracaibo, which is really just an extension of the Gulf of Venezuela, which itself is really just an extension of the Caribbean Sea. "He's here," I say. "I just know it. Torden Detonde is here, and he's going to be either at or very close to those GPS coordinates my brother dug up from cellphone records. We have to be careful, and we have to be ready. But we also have to be thorough. He can't be trusted, and you know he's up to no good."

"You still have Orkan's Quell Node?" Pers asks, chewing a bite of food.

I shake my head.

"Damn. I would've liked to use that on Torden."

"I can do to Torden the same thing I did to the Bissets," I say, probably sounding a bit smug.

"You sure that'll work on him? We know the Quell Node does."

I shrug. I'm not sure it'll work, but I am certain I'll try. But something else is on my mind. "What if he's surrounded by a hundred armed guards?" Sure, I've killed before. I'm not exactly proud of it, though, and I'd prefer to keep my body count as low as I can.

Sighing, Percival drops his fork. "I understand, Lyn. Really. But if regulars have chosen to be his army, then they get what they get. We can try to swoop in, fly out, things they can't do, but if that becomes impossible, we have to fight our way through. If he's guarded by people who are anywhere near as crazy as the ones we saw in Switzerland, well, shoot first, ask questions later."

I have visions of deadly lightning springing from my fingertips, and Percival's. *Right*, I think. *Our way. Step right up and see the great electromagicians! They can use their amazing powers for... hm... levitating and killing people with bolts of electricity! And Torden thinks we're somehow superior?*

29

LAID TO WASTE

Late the next morning, we head south through the city, Luis at the wheel. "Did you see the show last night?"

Luis is apparently trying to make friendly conversation, but I have no idea what he means. Also, it begins to dawn on me that Luis might know much more than just Transactional English. "I'm sorry, *show*? What show?"

He waggles one finger toward roof of the car, or maybe the sky above. "The lightning. It was a good show last night."

Lightning last night? Damn, wish we had seen it. Up close and personal. Always good to get a charge. "No, sorry. We were very tired. You know, jet lag."

"Ah, too bad. Next time," he says, turning his focus back to guiding us past the central part of town, then down through seemingly endless rows of residential houses.

Compared to New York City, most of Maracaibo definitely has a more flat and sprawling feel. After a million or so houses — no, I didn't count — we enter a more industrial area. Some large structures go by on our left, and even with my rudimentary understanding of Spanish, I get the meaning on one sign: *Planta Eléctrica Rafael Urdaneta*. Electrical plant, of course. I point it out to Percival.

He looks down at his phone, following our progress toward a cluster of blue dots. "Shoulda known this guy would take up residence in a place near the power station."

As we travel along, I begin to think the GPS coordinates my brother sent are leading us somewhere quite specific: the very, very center of absolutely nowhere. Out the windows, all I see for miles is scrubland and dirt, with only the occasional ramshackle building along the route. Finally, at Percival's urging, Luis turns left onto a side road between some of the more dense vegetation. "You can let us out here," Pers says.

Luis stops the car, but turns around to give us a skeptic, almost worried look. "Here? There's nothing around."

Thankfully, Percival had the sense to come up with an alibi of sorts. He flashes one of his patented perfect smiles. "Sure, there is, up ahead. Along the lake, there are some houses. We have a friend who lives in one."

Luis isn't convinced. "Okay, but I can just drive you directly there. The *lago* is a more than a kilometer away."

Percival keeps smiling, laying on his brand of charm. "Nah," he says, waving a hand in a friendly but dismissive way. "We haven't seen this friend in a while, and I want to surprise him. If he sees a taxi cab rolling up, he might figure it out before we have a chance to knock on his door and see the surprise on his face ourselves."

"You are sure? Should I wait here for you?"

"No, please, don't. I'm not sure how long we'll be here. It could be hours." I add a smiling nod of my own, trying to make Luis believe everything is great.

He pauses, thinking over the situation. "There are not going to be any other taxis this far south, so let me do this. Maybe ten or twelve kilometers back, there is a market I know, and it has a little cafe. I will go there and have a coffee, and perhaps lunch. When you need a ride, call me, and if I'm still at the cafe, it will be much quicker to come get you. And, you know, cheaper for you than me driving all the way from the city and back. Some other drivers around here may not be ones you can trust."

It's too kind of a gesture to turn down, so we happily agree, watching as Luis backs out on the main road and heads north. I mean, he has no idea that we're completely capable of defending ourselves in any normal dangerous situation — mugging, robbery, abduction — and me being from Rich Family Hopkins, I'm not exactly worried about the fare either.

Once the car is no more than a dot kicking up a wall of dust in the distance, we head southwest, away from the lake, in the direction Percival's map is guiding us. Luckily for us, there are enough dense bushes and larger trees that we aren't just walking up to the location completely exposed. Also, the trees give us a little relief from the relentless heat of the sun. The only problem is, the foliage blocks any hint of a breeze, and the humidity is about a billion percent. Plus, there are bugs. Lots of bugs.

Finally, Pers stops, pointing toward two structures: a small, simple house, and a much larger concrete monstrosity behind. Both look like they might fall down if a hummingbird flapped its wings nearby. "Well, this is where all those cellphone records point, so if Torden isn't here, then we're wasting our time in South America. But why would he be here? This place is a dump."

A similarity dawns on me. "Remember the pavilion, back in New York? That place had about the same kind of look, post-modern pre-condemned."

"True," Pers says with a shrug. "And I suppose if he was way out here in some kind of palace, that would draw a lot of attention."

"Exactly." I glance back and forth from the house to the concrete structure. "Which one first?"

"The house," he says without hesitation. "If we go into the big building, anyone in the house can cut us off from behind. So we start with the closer one. Besides, it's smaller. Think of it as a warmup."

Once more, Percival flashes his perfect teeth at me, and I do something that I realize I need to do more often. I grab him and give him a quick but passionate kiss. "If we survive all of this, I'm leaving the world of the High Order, Prime Order, and whatever the hell Torden is behind. I need a break from this shit."

"Agreed," he says, eyes still sparkling in that way they do after a particularly good kiss.

———

As quietly as we can, we approach the house. If they have cameras or guards posted, I can't locate either. It just seems like a dilapidated old shack. Near the front door, Pers carefully glances into a dust-covered window, then turns to me and shrugs. "Maybe this isn't the place," he whispers. "I see no one."

"Let's go in and see what we can find."

Percival tries the knob, and it turns with ease, thankfully not making a sound. The door, however, creaks a little as he swings it inward, so I keep my attention swiveling all around, making sure no one suddenly sneaks up on us. Nothing.

We enter the house and find it dark and full of shadows compared to the sunlit outdoors. For a moment, I hope it's cooler inside, but the humidity remains, as does the majority of the heat. The place is cluttered with *things*, all seemingly piled upon other things. Books, papers, and scrawled notes sit atop too many chairs, tables, and cabinets for the small space. The layout seems simple enough: past the front room, there's a short, open hallway to a small kitchen. Two doors stem off to the right of the hall, leading to what I predict will be a couple of bedrooms or a bed and a bath. I'm right on the second count. Sure, we have a seriously tense SWAT-team-style moment before opening each of the two doors, but there's no one home. We end up in the kitchen. "I know this is where the GPS points were," Pers says, sounding apologetic.

"We haven't checked the other building yet. He could still be there. Let's not let our guard down. I — hold on," I say, stepping toward a sink half-full of dirty dishes. Standing to the left of the sink is an empty wine bottle. An empty *French* wine bottle. "He's here. Or at least he was. Unless a lot of people in this barely populated part of Venezuela drink *Châteauneuf-du-Pape*." And yes, I probably butcher the pronunciation. Sue me.

Pers nods. "All right, then we need a plan of attack for the big building out back." From the darkened kitchen, we stare out a small window toward the other structure, analyzing it. Percival points. "I see a metal door on the far left side and the same on the far right. We seem to have lucked out — no windows facing this direction, so hopefully no one's seen us yet. We could split up, each take a side, then work our way back together in the center of the building?"

"I'm not exactly the queen of infiltration techniques, so yeah, okay, if you say so. But power up *first*, and be ready."

"Hey, hon," he says with casual confidence, tiny zaps of electricity already pulsing between his fingertips as he begins to glow. "Remember, you juiced me up — I'm a level 10 EM. I'm ready for anything now." This time, he leans in to kiss me, and it's electric. In multiple ways. "You go right, I'll go left. Meet in the middle. Any trouble, make as much freaking noise as you can and I'll be there on the double."

"Same goes for you, then," I say.

"Deal."

We slip out of the house by its front door, then each take our side to circle toward the concrete building. Furtively scanning the yard between structures, I'd say it's 25 meters or so, but it's all open space. Glancing toward Pers, I see him hold out three fingers, starting a countdown. When the last finger drops and he gives a quick fist pump, we both run, reaching our respective doors at about the same time. We pause. Listening, waiting. Nothing.

I increase the flow of electricity through my body until my skin is humming with power and I reach for the knob as Percival echoes my move at the other end of the building. Then he nods, and we each quickly swing our door open.

Though both are miraculously unlocked, mine, unfortunately shrieks as metal scrapes on metal, then stops, only halfway open. Again we wait. Again, nothing. There's enough of an opening for me to continue, so I gesture to Pers to keep going and we both slip inside.

The room I enter is a stark contrast to the cluttered and dim house we just left. Here, high windows on the side walls allow a lot of light in, and everything I see appears to be clean and new. The most notable aspect of the room is that it's divided in two sections — a smaller, office-like area where I've just entered, and a much larger lab or maybe factory space in the back. The two are separated by a floor-to-ceiling plexiglass partition, and smack in the middle of that is a revolving door, like I've just walked up to some fancy New York hotel. Only there's no doorman, no bellhop, no one at all, and this revolving door is as clear as the wall. If I were to guess — and really, what other option do I have? — I think the entire larger room in the back appears to be some kind of airtight work space.

Through the transparent dividing wall, I can see another door along the left side, which means that's my way to continue into the heart of the building and get back face-to-face with Percival. I push forward, through the revolving door, and into the rear chamber.

And that's when I realize what the machinery is that I'm looking at. A chair, connected by a ton of wires to a bank of computers; the same setup we found Torden and the Bissets using in Paris. The same setup that sucked the life out of my friend, Hayden. My anger flares and I almost use my power to destroy the entire place in that instant, until I realize that we still have an incomplete picture of what we're up against. Destruction will have to wait.

I open the side door and find a small, boxy space with another door on the opposite side. I step in, walking quietly to the far door, and I grab for its knob to open it. Small problem: there is no knob.

On the wall to the left of the door is a square button, illuminated by a dull internal light. I push it.

Suddenly the door behind me snaps closed and a hear a loud click as I'm locked in the space. *Shit.* There's a whooshing sound above me, and then suddenly I am being sprayed with some kind of mist. All along the walls, long purple lights begin to glow. *Great. I'm locked in a box, being decontaminated. That's not too ominous.* At least I *hope* I'm just being decontaminated and not, you know, gassed to death. Because EM power is great and all, and sure, I recently figured out how to stop bullets. But I still have to breathe, and I'm definitely not immune to poison.

Whatever was misting over me stops, and I don't feel faint or ill or anything, so maybe it's okay. I hear another click and the door I had been trying to open is suddenly illuminated by a small overhead light. I push on it and I'm relieved to find it glides easily to reveal a much larger space.

I'm even more relieved when a door opposite me opens and Percival steps out, blinking away his surprise. "Well, that was weird as shit."

"You can say that again. Find anything?" I ask.

He raises his hands, palms up. "Storage. I think. Lots of bits and pieces. Tech stuff. Computers, metal arms, tubes. All kinds of strange crap, but no people."

Finally, I look around the new room we've entered. "Speaking of strange crap... what is all *this*?"

The entire back half of the huge room looks like it's an automated car assembly factory, with giant robot arms on the left and right, and a round disk in the floor that appears to be a rotating section. On that disk between the robot arms, however, there's nothing.

"Maybe Torden's giving up on all his wacko EM plans and now he's gonna make cheap hatchbacks in Venezuela?"

I chuckle, but quickly our confusion dries up any sort of amusement. I nod back toward the way I came. "I found one of those contraptions, like in Paris. The kind he used on Hayden."

"So, this is — or was — Torden's place."

"Yep," I say, sternly.

Looking around, Pers twists his face in a pondering grimace. "What do you want to do about it, given that he's not here?"

I look at him with steel in my eyes. "I want to burn it to the ground."

He nods, several times, briskly. "All right. I'm down with that. Start here, and work backwards the way we each came?"

"Sure." I take a deep breath. And then, knowing that all the machinery around us has a breaking point — a point where it will overload it and start a fire — I thrust out both hands and dazzlingly bright arcs of blue electricity shoot toward the control panel of the robot contraption on my side of the room. Percival does the same on his side, and it isn't long before there are sparks, smoke, and, finally, spreading flames.

From there, we work rapidly, knowing that we're currently inside a building on fire. Percival runs to the door where he entered and disappears. A few seconds later, I do the same, and once I'm inside the little decontamination box, I'm no longer interested in staying quiet. I fire at the door lock system on the far side, running for the exit.

And I *bounce* off the sealed door. "What th—?" I shove at it again, but nothing. Well, damn it, I'm definitely not burning to death inside this little chamber, especially if Pers might be trapped in the other one. I burn brightly, blindingly, sending a massive amount of energy into the wall, the door, anything electric I can find, and finally, something snaps and the door feebly opens, just a crack. It's enough for me to know the lock is toast, so I lean into the door and push into the far room.

Once more I fire bolts, this time with a mixture of both glee at destroying one of the devices Torden Detonde uses to steal lives, and a sorrow for the loss of those lives. Nothing escapes my power, and this room is soon on fire as well. I push through the clear revolving door, into the office, give the computers there a quick fry, just for good measure, then slip out into the bright light of day.

Already, black smoke is beginning to billow into the sky over the roofline. I stare at the opposite door, Percival's door, waiting for it to open.

One second. Two. Three. It doesn't move.

"Shit, he's trapped," I say aloud, running for the other door and pushing inside.

I expect the room to be free of fire, but it isn't. Percival has been here, has already set it ablaze. As if to confirm that fact, I see the door to his decontamination chamber is ajar. *Where the hell is he?* Inside my head, I shout out with EM communication, "Pers, where d'you go?"

No answer. The smoke burns at my eyes and nostrils, and hurriedly, I run back outside...

...to find a man in head-to-toe camouflage holding a long black assault rifle, its business end pointed at me. Behind large, reflective sunglasses, he smiles at me, smugly. "There you are," he says, with what sounds like a British accent.

"What the hell did you do with Percival?"

I begin to raise my hands, but before I move an inch, the guard menacingly gestures with the rifle. "Not so fast, princess. Hate if I had to damage such a pretty thing with this."

Only he doesn't know what I know. Bullets can't hurt me. Rather than lunge forward with EM power, I cringe downward, making myself small.

"See? That's better. Good for you for seeing the sensible way."

And then I pulse out a bubble of energy, doming it around me. He must think it's an attack, and he has a seriously itchy trigger finger. Immediately he fires. But the bullets all bounce away.

Unluckily for him, one bounces straight back, destroying his kneecap in a sickening burst of blood and flesh. He falls, and the gun flails upward.

It's enough.

I dart forward, sending a zap of electricity — just a bit — into the one hand still holding the weapon, and he pulls it away reflexively. I can see the flesh there is already charred and bubbling. I grab the gun, but of course, he has it strapped over his shoulder. He starts to reach with his good hand to reclaim the assault rifle, but another quick flare of power to that hand makes him think better of the idea. "Take off the strap."

"Hold on, hold on," he says.

"Take it off *now*!"

And so, to his credit, this Brit guard with a blown out knee and two burned hands does the smart thing, wiggling his body along the ground to allow the strap to slide over his head. I quickly swing the gun around to point it at his head. "Where is my friend?"

"He's gone," the man says, his answer frustratingly obvious in its simplicity.

I grunt with rage. "What does that mean? Hurry up. My finger's getting tired and might just squeeze."

"Well, I'll tell you this. You're a lot more careful than this Percival you mention. First, he didn't see me in the back of the storeroom, and then, when he came out, he just stood by that door, waiting for you to come through the other way. Wasn't hard for me to, you know, knock him out with the back of that gun."

Ugh, Pers, you big dummy. You should've been more careful. You shouldn't have just been looking for me. I feel guilty. He'd better be all right.

"Okay, then what? Where d'you put him?"

The man laughs. "*I* didn't put him anywhere. But I did make a phone call, and he got picked up."

"That doesn't make any sense. We're in the middle of nowhere."

"Oh, he didn't get picked up in a car, if that's what you're asking. He got picked up by *him*." The guard uses one burned hand to gesture like a plane flying in and then flying away.

Him? Shit. Torden, of course. The bastard flew in using EM power and was able to fly Percival out the same way. But how? I was only delayed in that chamber a few moments. *No, he didn't call Torden then. He must have called as soon as Percival left the storeroom to meet me.* "To where? Where are they going?"

"No idea. I'm just the production facility guard. The only one left behind after they finished up here."

I'm so confused. But that center room was obviously set up to build something, and knowing Torden, that something was awful, and it put Percival in grave danger. "Which direction did they go? Tell me that and maybe I won't put a bullet in your head."

The guy thinks about it, and I realize he could always just lie. But the allegiance of a soldier of fortune can be a fickle thing, and he answers. "North. Back toward the city, I guess."

"Give me your phone."

"I can't do th—"

I'm done with the runaround. I cut him off, spinning the rifle butt down to slam into his forehead, hard, knocking him out, and smashing those stupid-looking sunglasses at the same time.

Rifling through his pockets, I find his phone and bring up the last number dialed.

30

AN ACE UP THE SLEEVE

"Well, that was fast," Torden says with a tone that sounds obnoxiously like glee.

"Hurt Percival, and I will find you anywhere in the world. But I won't just kill you, I'll take your power away and make you feel *real* pain." As an opening remark, that pretty much sums up my mood.

Torden seems to ignore the threat. "Is Jeffery still alive? The guard whose phone you're using to call me right now."

"Yes. But he'll remember meeting me, I promise," I bark.

Torden just laughs. "And there you go. That's your problem, Ms. Hopkins. You're too nice. You let me live, when you could have easily killed me. And I can assure you, Jeffery was trained *not* to leave living people behind. If you only had more... *conviction*... maybe your parents would still be alive."

Now I'm seething. "You bastard. Why did you do it?"

"Because, child. All of these lemmings keep getting in my way. The High Order, the Prime Order. All these old guard that can't see what's real."

"And what's that?"

"It is that the time is *now*. There's no more time to sit around, waiting for electromagicians to band together, waiting for some *kumbaya* moment. It's never going to happen. The High Order will be in hiding forever, and the Prime Order will never get enough momentum to reveal themselves to the world. That why they both need to be dismantled."

"Oh, and I bet you're just the guy to do it, right? The only one who can." I'm so mad, I punch a fist in the air, probably far too obvious a reference to my current level of futility.

"That is *exactly* who I am." On the other end of the line, I hear something like a smug sigh.

I nod to myself, trying to return to the now. To what's important. "You don't want Percival. You've told me that yourself. You want *me*. You want the things only *I* can do."

"Well, one has to make compromises sometimes. Perhaps I'll get your abilities later. For now, Percival should provide a good source of power renewal."

"If you do that, you'll never get what I have."

Once again, Torden chuckles. "And how exactly would you prevent me, Lyn?"

I reach a snap decision. "Because if you kill Percival, I'll kill myself, and what I have will die with me. You'll never get it."

"Hm," he says, sounding truly perplexed by my words. "Interesting." There's a long pause while Torden thinks of how to address it. "Then I suppose we're at a bit of an impasse. I have sought your power for so long that I'm unwilling to give it up so frivolously, but I can't just return Percival to you, alive and well. So…"

"So, what?"

"I suppose you'll have to come find us. Goodbye *Lightning Hopkins*."

"Hold on—"

I hear the beginnings of another laugh when the call is cut off.

"Damn it!" I shout to no one at all.

———

I CAN'T DECIDE. Half of me wants to follow Torden's lead and use EM power to fly back north, but the other half says that would mostly be futile, considering I don't know where I'm going exactly. Plus, I wonder if that nice driver, Luis, is still sitting at some cafe hoping for a fare from us — or me only this time, I should say — back to the city. In the end, I figure some time rolling along in a car will let me sift through my thoughts.

"*Aló*," Luis says, answering the call. I ask him if he's still nearby. "Yes! Should I come to where I dropped you off?"

"Please. But... it will just be me this time. Um. My friend decided to stay here for a little while."

"Sure. Okay. I will see you very soon."

A short while later, I'm standing around on that side road that leads to the lake, pretty bored and wondering if I should've just done things *my* special way. Then I hear the hum of a distant engine and lean out into the main road to see a column of dust growing closer. When he finally pulls over, Luis looks genuinely happy to see me. Hot, exhausted, and alone in a remote part of a country I don't know much about, I'm genuinely happy to see him, too.

———

EVEN AFTER 15 minutes of driving, I can't think of what to do next except call my brother and ask for help, so I do. He's the one who told us where to look in the first place, so maybe he'll have new ideas. "Hey, Kevin."

"Lyn. What happened? Are you okay?"

I'm keenly aware that Luis, while very nice, can hear everything I say, so I have to use a bit of code to get my message across. "I'm fine. Percival is... with a friend, for now. Are there, um, any other places you can think of in Maracaibo city, or at least north of where I just was, that might be, um, also good to visit?" Hopefully Luis is ignoring me, because my encrypted message sounds ridiculous to my ears. From my vantage, he seems to just be following the road, his head swaying back and forth with every bump, in time with a colorful little knitted decoration hanging from the rearview mirror. I wonder for a moment which of his kids made it for him.

Kevin thinks a moment before replying. "I mean, the GPS locations I sent you were, by far, the most likely places."

"What do you mean by *most likely*?" I ask.

"Well, you know, people travel around, and they bring their cellphones everywhere. Just because you talk on the phone from a gas station or supermarket, doesn't mean that's where someone should go looking for you. Those are usually one-offs, and not worth pursuing."

"And the ones you sent were, what? Used often?"

"Yes." *Damn.* It seems like a dead end. I'm quiet for a while, trying to think if there's any angle.

"You still there?" Kevin asks.

"Yeah, yeah. Just thinking." But what? What miracle idea am I going to come up with? Torden Detonde flew off with Percival to *somewhere* north of me in Venezuela. Or was that even right? Was he just *somewhere north*? That narrowed it down to, hm, let's say, all of North America. And the Arctic. Maybe Torden went to the North Pole. Maybe Torden is Santa Claus. "Shit."

"Can you tell me what happened at least, Lyn?" Kevin asks.

I change the subject, to inform him of what I can and can't say out loud. "Oh, yeah, I'm just getting a taxi ride back to the city right now. Same driver, Luis." Confirming that he can hear me, Luis waves and glances at me in the rearview when he hears his name.

"Got it. You can't talk now."

"Right," I say, still thinking what might help find Torden's new home base. *Ah, damn. That's the answer right there. In front of my face all along.* "Hey, Kev, can you sort those GPS locations by date?"

"Of course."

"Then can you tell me some of the more *recent* ones? I'm afraid one of our, uh, friends might have moved recently."

"Oh really," Kevin says. "Well, that may make a big difference. Hold on." As usual, with Kevin on the phone, I can faintly hear a keyboard clacking away. He's never far from a desk or a computer.

"There are four calls near the end of the records we got from the Bissets. They've gone dark since you dealt with them, or maybe they have new phones I'm not aware of. Anyway, in both cases, two GPS coordinates are nearly overlapping. So we have two small areas to investigate, or else we have no more data to work with."

"Send me that info. I'll start there."

"Okay, but Lyn. If he knows you're in Venezuela, he'll certainly be laying a trap for you."

"Well, luckily, I have an ace up my sleeve."

"The thing you did to the Bissets? So you told me. But Lyn. Torden Detonde is... well, I doubt he's going to be on the same level as the Bissets. He's going to be much, much stronger."

I gulp. The Bissets were essentially no one to me — a couple of old people who were basically evil from our first meeting. Torden is something else. From as far back as I can remember, he was said to be a trusted mentor. A peaceful leader, revered in our community, even though I always felt strange around him. He was loved, and he was strong. Then we exposed him for doing things no High Order EM could ever be permitted to do, creating Stickmen, killing people, some being my friends. And yet, even though I chased him and hated him and helped catch him and wanted to see him punished, I also spent time just traveling and talking with him. All of those things change a perspective. Am I worried that, all along, he was learning about me, finding something to use against me? Maybe. Am I worried that a 200-year-old EM knows more and can do more than I would ever imagine? Yes. Am I worried that I could die, or watch as my abilities and power get slowly sucked away? Damn straight. But I can't say any of those things to Kevin. He'd do everything in his power to stop me. So I lie. "Doesn't matter. I like the challenge."

For a second, I almost convince myself I'm ready.

31

I AM THE TOUCHSTONE

Two locations, one me.

And the longer I take to find Torden, the more likely something bad happens to Percival. I... I couldn't live if that happened. Sure, I've spent years pretending not to be interested, then more time pushing him away. Not anymore. I will do *anything*. He's everything I want and need, and I've already lost too much. Far too much.

I'll tear a hole in the earth and crush Torden down in its black veins of rock, if that's what I have to do.

I decide to start with the nearest location. All this hunting for people in strange places has kinda made me an expert in using the map on my phone, which is about the same as being an expert at walking or breathing, given the complexity of the task. Still, I find myself zooming and swiping, thinking of the best approach angle. Do most people think about *approach angle* when using their phone map? I hope not.

I freeze.

All of this is just more of me avoiding the obvious.

Percival.

Why can't I focus on the one thing that actually matters? Torden has Percival.

Could I live a thousand years and let Torden live, if I never heard him or saw him again?

Yes.

Could I live another second if Torden hurt Percival?

No.

"Luis, can you pull over for a minute? I need to change our destination."

"Yes, Miss Lyn," he says, gliding to a halt along the side of the dusty road. We've just begun the northward trek through the endless suburbs, but there are plenty of dirt patches beside the road to choose from.

"Here," I say, holding my phone out to show the dot of where I want to go. It's not exactly where Kevin's data said to go, just close enough.

Luis is silent.

Oh shit, what did I do wrong? But of course, I know. How many American tourists come to Maracaibo, then ask to be driven to these oddball remote locations? My guess is precisely none. Sure, I could probably get away with one, but now? The second time it must seem very strange. Other people probably want to go to the lake or one of the big churches we've passed. Me? Remote dirt road, and don't ask questions, thank you very much. Suspicious? Yup.

"Are you sure about this location, Miss Lyn?" he asks hesitantly.

"Yes, that's definitely the right location," I say, trying to sound confident, as if my request was perfectly normal. Once again, he's quiet. I try to play it off. "Is something wrong, Luis?"

"It's just that there is nothing there," he says, the unease clear in his tone. "I do not feel right driving you to this place and leaving you there alone."

I'm at a loss for a counterargument, but every moment I delay "Can I trust you?" I blurt. "I mean, I want to, and I think I can, but I can't say for sure. Can I trust you, Luis?"

Luis looks down at his hands resting on the steering wheel, pausing a moment. "Miss Lyn, my job may not be something like president or businessman or anything much, but to me it is important. I know I am just taking you where you want to go, but getting you there safely... bringing you back safely... These things are important to me."

"And I appreciate that. I — I can promise you I will be safe, but I must go to this location."

"But I have to ask why," he says. He fumbles for the words in English. "If you are... making crime or something, I will not look away and let it happen in my country."

"I can assure I'm not. But if I was *stopping* people who were making crime?"

There is another long pause. "Then I would be proud to drive you," he says.

"Please hurry," I say. I think the desperation in my eyes is the final thing Luis needs to be convinced.

———

OUR DESTINATION IS east of the city, on the far side of Lake Maracaibo, which means we have to travel across the massive, miles-long structure of General Urdaneta Bridge. It's like nothing I've ever seen before, span after lengthy span, stepping between high towers striped with cables to support the road. We have the windows down despite our speed, and the hot air whips my hair around into tangles and knots. I don't care. At least when the air is moving, it's less oppressive. I glance up as we pass below one of the towers and see heat lightning in the clouds overhead. *Not so great for a charge. Too hard to get to it, way up there.*

The eastern shore of the lake features houses close to the water, then not much else after that. Quickly, we're deep in a remote area where the passing houses diminish from occasional to almost nonexistent. As we approach the dot on my phone map, I realize we haven't seen another soul in quite some time.

Finally, Luis guides the car to park in the shade of a dense, tall row of thorny bushes. "This time, I will wait," he says.

"I'd actually appreciate that. If there's no one here, I have another place to look," I tell him. "But... if there *is* someone here, well, there may be..." How am I going to phrase this? "There may be a bit of a struggle. I can assure you that I'm well trained and capable. Please don't risk endangering yourself by coming closer." Luis looks like a man torn between chivalry and wondering why he was the unlucky bastard dragged into all this. "Look," I say, pulling out my wallet. "These are all the euros I have." I hold the wad of bills out to him.

Luis's eyes bug out. I didn't bother counting, but imagine that I'm holding at least ten times what I owe him, or more. "Miss Lyn, I cannot accept this from you, and... and I will not be bribed."

I shake my head. "It's not a bribe. It's just... an *advance*. Whatever happens here, I'm going to need to either go back to the hotel or go to another location. If I ask you to wait around, that's time you could be getting other fares, making other money. So I'm offering you this as an incentive to wait for me. If you want to give me change back later, that's fine."

Then Luis, a man I've known for such a short period of time, gives me a look of parental concern deeper than anything I can ever recall seeing from my real parents. "Okay, Miss Lyn. But be very careful. Unfortunately, not everyone in my country can be trusted."

I smile and nod, stepping out of the car before he can see the tears welling in my eyes. "That's true in every country, Luis. Trust me."

———

EARLY AFTERNOON, deep in the scrub. The greenery hides me well, but once more cuts any sort of breeze down to almost nothing. It's miserably hot and humid, and I don't look but assume I've got some lovely pit stains growing on my shirt. Whatever. The hell with how I look. I need to find Percival and set him free. Then we can deal with Torden. Together.

Up ahead is a low structure, one story, wider by far than it is tall. I'm approaching it on a diagonal, able to see the front and one short side where a noisy generator is running. Beside that stands a skeletal tower, several times higher than the corrugated metal roof of the building itself.

It's probably a trap, I think. *It's probably a trap*. I don't know what good it is to repeat this to myself, but still I do it. I hope my angle of approach and the sound of the generator give me some element of surprise, but I can't be sure. Once more I shake my head at the thought of me rationalizing an approach angle.

I wait several minutes, watching, in a dense tangle of bushes maybe 50 meters from the structure, but there's no motion. Slowly, quietly, I step out and start to cover the open area to reach the building.

Still nothing.

I crouch next to the generator and wait.

Nothing.

I realize that the noise is keeping *me* from hearing anything else, so I start to move, seeking a new place where I can watch the front door.

And the muzzle of a hand gun is pressed against my left temple.

"Welcome, Lyn Hopkins," an old familiar voice says, very close to the back of my head. Rand Haldor, Torden's eternal second in command. "Don't move now, please," he says calmly, almost serenely. "I'd hate for anything to happen to you just yet." I sense him fumble for something with his other hand, then he's talking again, but not to me. "I have her here with me. Shall I bring her to you?" A pause. "Very well. We will arrive very soon." I feel movement again, probably Rand putting the phone back in his pocket.

So I don't wait.

Guessing, I thrust one fist backward in a low arc, as hard as I can, and I strike pay dirt: Rand's crotch.

The man lets out an almost wet sounding *oof* as he falls backward onto his ass. Quickly, I spin around, trying to locate the gun. Yeah, I can make a bulletproof shield, but it won't help me much if the gun is inside with me. He's still holding it in his left hand, but for the moment, its business end is pointing off toward the trees. Even in his pain, with his face twisted in a grimace, he sees my intention, and swings the gun back toward me. But I rise and kick at his hand, knocking the weapon free and sending it skittering in the dirt some distance away.

For a moment, Rand and I stare at each other, frozen.

Then he quickly fills with power and launches himself into the air, racing east and away. A second later, I do the same.

We're two streaking blue glows high above a nearly deserted landscape. I have no idea if anyone sees us, or what they might think if they do, but I am not letting this man escape again. He was there, in Paris, when they turned Hayden into a burned husk. He's been behind Torden and every horrible thing that man has done since the beginning. Rand suddenly zips left, and I alter course to follow.

Now we're like two fighter jets, him trying to outmaneuver me, and me trying to keep him in sight. So far, it's easy; the ground is flat. But ahead, I can see densely forested mountains approaching. If he reaches those, he could use them for cover, making the chase much harder for me. I try to speed up, but we're both at or near our maximum. Still I push myself, and I gain. Again, Rand makes a sharp, sudden turn, this time right and down, and I follow, hot behind him.

"What's the point? You can't do anything to me but waste your power!" Rand yells as he once more changes direction.

"Oh really?" I reply, and a moment later answer his question physically rather than verbally. I slam into him sideways, sending him spiraling into the air. I don't know how bad it might have hurt, but I can tell right away, it pisses him off.

Rand gets control of his movement, coming to a floating stop maybe a thousand feet in the air. I pause slightly lower. We glare at each other.

And then Rand dives right for me, and honestly, I almost laugh. Rand Haldor is over 150 years old, and now he's coming for me, to fight me with his fists. I steady myself, ready to snap his old bones like twigs.

Which is when Rand's fist catches me in the stomach and I feel an explosion of pain. *Holy shit, that hurt!*

I punch back, striking the bridge of his nose, which immediately breaks the skin and sends blood flying in a splatter toward the distant earth below. But he doesn't hesitate, knocking my head back with an uppercut to the chin like being hit with a hammer.

Of all the ways I expected this to go down, fist fight in midair was not one of them.

I'm no trained fighter, so maybe my next move is dirty, but who cares? I kick forward, trying to give his most delicate of parts a second taste of pain. That seemed to get him pretty good the first time. But Rand is quick, much quicker than he looks, and he's able to grab my foot and flip me head over heels backward. When I regain control of myself, I see a blue streak heading for the mountains. I lean forward and shoot toward him, unwilling to let him simply escape.

Somehow Rand is tapping his reserves and going faster than ever before. He's going to reach the range well before me, and then I'm sure he'll do a series of turns until finding him in the messy terrain will be damned near impossible.

Desperate, I clench both fists and will myself to use every ounce of my abilities to speed up. I become a comet in the afternoon sky, going so fast that anyone below who might see it would swear a meteor was about to crash into the earth. It's only when I get near that I realize what I've done — my speed is so great that Rand is helpless to outrun me. I slam into his body with such force that both of us are tossed and tangled, flipping and spinning, and the harsh terrain rises swiftly to meet us.

A moment later, we're both battered into the rocky landscape, tumbling and swirling until we finally come to a halt on a wide flat plateau.

I try to lift myself off the ground, but realize that everything hurts. Sure, I'm alive, and I'm sure Rand is, too, and our EM power probably saved us from being crushed by the impact, but it didn't make it a walk in the park. I wonder if I have broken bones, but push myself up anyway. It's time.

Staggering to my feet, I watch as Rand, too, rises with great effort. We face each other like gunslingers in some old black and white movie.

"It's over," I say, the exhaustion clear in my voice.

Rand Haldor laughs at me. "What do you know about *anything*, little girl? Nothing is *over*. You can batter me some more if you like, but there's nothing else you can do."

"You're wrong. I can take everything away from you. Even your power. All of it."

Rand freezes, eyeing me suspiciously, disbelievingly. "Ridiculous," he spits. "You don't hold the Touchstone of Mount Hachiro. You're just a silly girl, and everyone you've ever loved has been taken from you. Now run home before you get yourself hurt again."

His words sting, mostly because they're true. I have lost everyone. Maybe I am a silly girl for getting this deep into things I don't understand. But I'm not leaving without Percival. "Tell me where they are."

"Oh, definitely," Rand says. "Or shall I just drive you there myself? Please, stop being so foolish. If Torden wants you to know where he is, he'll call for you himself."

"Then you're of no use to me."

"Well," Rand says, smiling. A drip of blood slips down one cheek from a cut below his eye. "That's the first accurate thing you've said. I am of no use to you, because you are nothing to me." His sneer causes the blood droplet to alter course, creating an angled streak on his face that looks like insanity.

"And now *you* are nothing to anyone at all." I close my eyes, reaching out with my power.

Immediately, I realize my mistake. There's no one else. No Percival, no parents. To make my special magic happens, I need a very powerful EM nearby, like an energy source. But here, it's just Rand and me.

Rand cocks his head slightly, giving me a confused look. Then, without warning, his face falls. He feels something.

At the same moment, I realize that I do, too.

But how?

I'm... Oh my God, is this even possible? I'm tapping Rand's power. How can I tap his power in order to remove his power? It seems like a paradox. Still, something is definitely happening. I only wonder how far it will go, like at some point the universe will catch on to the fact that this *shouldn't work.*

Rand stares at his own outstretched hands in disbelief. "What are you doing to me?" He sounds almost feral, and I both feel and see him pull himself inward, preparing to flee.

He looks up to the sky, but nothing happens.

All of his EM power is busy. There's none left for flying.

Under my direction, Rand Haldor's electromagic abilities are being used... to remove his electromagic abilities. "Stop it! Get away from me, you damned woman!" He staggers, but even walking is hard in the throes of what's happening.

"Oh, now I'm a woman? Nice of you to notice, finally. I thought you and Torden just called me *girl.*"

He answers with nothing but an animal grunt, still trying to stumble away from me.

It's too late — I feel the source of my extra power run out, just at the same moment I feel Rand's abilities are completely destroyed. The job is done, and, of all things, done with the very thing that was taken away.

As if struck in the back of the head, Rand falls forward, face first onto the rocky ground. He screams. He writhes on the ground. "What have you done?" His voice is high pitched.

I walk forward and toe into his side, forcing him to roll over onto his back. Then I crouch down and rifle through his pockets until I find his phone, snatching it up and tucking it into my back pocket.

I scan the area. We're on a plateau in the middle of a remote mountain range. To the west, the drop-off is steep. Every other direction looks like a difficult hike out at best. Will Rand make it out alive?

Who cares?

"Go to hell, Lyn Hopkins!" he says, spittle flying from his raving mouth. He's crying now, clearly aware that he's not the man he was moments before.

I think about my next stop: wherever Torden Detonde is hiding. It's probably some version of hell, so on that point, I imagine Rand is mostly right. But it also might be the death of me, and if so, maybe the real hell is in my future. At this point, it's hard to care anymore.

"Sure thing. But I imagine you'll get there before me." With my lip curled in an unsympathetic snarl, I fill myself with power and shoot into the sky, flying west. The sun is past its peak now, and in the distance, brilliant flashes light the insides of the clouds. It's a mirror of me, a shell filled with electricity, begging to be set free.

32

MAN OR MACHINE

Luis is sleeping, reclined in the driver's seat of his car, parked in the shade by the side of the road. I almost hate to wake the poor man.

Instead of shaking him and embarrassing him, I scuff my boots as I approach on the dusty road. Thankfully, he hears it, blinks himself awake, and is sitting like nothing happened by the time I get near the car. Because nothing happened. What do I care if this guy gets some rest? I'd love to be getting some myself right now. I realize dimly how tired I am, not just from the day itself, though that's been plenty. I'm tired from everything that's happened in the recent history of my life. Back since... when?

I know. The guy in the gold muscle car that tried to shoot me in the Midwest. That was the beginning of it all. Before Torden knew he wanted to take my abilities, he thought killing me was the easiest option. That's where this all began. It feels like an eternity ago.

I have to finish things.

Today.

Because I think if I have another day of madness based on Torden Detonde in my life, it will actually drive me crazy.

And I want Pers back, more than I can say. More than I want to admit. No. Not anymore. If I get him back safely, I'll tell him how much I need him. This time I will.

"*Hola*, Miss Lyn," Luis says, alert and ready, but I see him wipe at one eye to remove the sleep still lingering there. How long have I been gone? Long enough for a good nap, I suppose, especially in this heat.

I wave. "Hi."

"Did… everything go as you hoped?" he asks tentatively. Overhead, there's a dull rumble as heat lightning leaps from cloud to cloud, making amorphous flashes in the sky.

"Yes," I reply with a sigh, because really, it's true. Rand is done. One more of Torden awful group taken out of the picture. And one left. "I have another place I need to go, but first, one more call to my brother. Can you give me another minute?"

"Miss Lyn, right now, I owe *you* money, so I will wait as long as you like." Luis smiles a warm smile, and I envy him. When this is done, all the things I'm involved with, he'll remain oblivious to the alternate world that exists all around him. He'll go back to his two kids and hopefully have a good life.

I walk away from the car, far enough for a little privacy, and pull out my phone.

Can I…? Can *we* possibly have a good life, after all this? Percival and me?

What are you talking about, Lyn? You know he's already dead.

No.

Stop it.

I can't think like that. Pers is alive and I'm going to get him back.

Something is buzzing in my ears. A voice.

"—lo? Hello, Lyn? Are you there?"

Crap. I dialed my brother and then immediately zoned out. "Hi, I'm here."

"Okay, well, that scared me. What the hell?" Kevin says.

"Sorry. I spaced for a second."

"All right. Tell me what's happening." I give him the short version of my encounter with Rand, and tell him I need to get to Torden before anything happens to Percival. He responds with a sort of noncommittal *Hm.* Then I tell him I have Rand's phone, and that Rand had been talking to Torden on it, the last call he made. "Give me the number." I fumble through the settings on the phone and dig up its number, then recite that to Kevin. "Totally new phone record system for that service. Give me a minute."

"Call you back or wait?"

"Lyn, how many times have you sat on the phone while I hacked some system?" he asks, sounding mildly annoyed.

"Um, a lot."

"Then have some faith. Hold the line."

Ever reliable, Kevin comes back much sooner than I expect. "It gels."

"Huh?"

"The last location, from Rand's last call. It gels with the point I already sent you. Torden is there."

"All right, thanks, Kev. Um, call you later, I guess." I can't say I sound terribly sure of it.

"Lyn," he says, more concerned than I've ever heard him before. "Maybe wait. Maybe let me get a group together, fly down to meet you..."

"No, I can't. Torden has Percival, and every second I wait is unbearable. If something were to happen to Pers..." I don't need to say any more.

"Okay. But remember this: you've taken care of three of the most powerful EMs on earth, rendered them harmless. Torden isn't the same as them, but I don't know that he's more than all three of them together. If you can overcome the Bissets and Rand, well..."

"Thanks," I say, my voice near empty. Kevin means well, but he can't say for sure what I might face. "I'll — I'll try to call again." That's it. Not call again *later*, just call again. As in *ever*. I tap the button to end the call.

And now there's nothing more to do. I pause a moment, as if I'm going to pray or meditate or somehow give myself a boost. But there's nothing. *Boy, getting recharged would've been a really good idea.* I reach inside. There's power there, and my Quotient means I can stretch it. But how far?

Time will tell.

———

WE START OFF DRIVING NORTHEAST, but once we get beyond a large cove branching from the lake, Luis guides us back toward the west. Back to the water. Bumping down dusty roads with the windows open, I realize the grit is getting everywhere — in my hair, mouth, eyes. My hands are covered with flecks of sand, and idly I rub my fingers against my thumb to dislodge it. I have a sense that something awful is about to happen, but I don't know what. Looking at the grit on my fingers, an old phrase comes to mind. *I can show you fear in a handful of dust.*

After a while bumping down dirt roads, we start to see houses once more — lots of houses lined in suburban rows. "Drop me off here," I tell Luis as we round a bend. It's a good distance from the dot on the map I showed him, and he knows it.

He pulls over, but it's an uneasy pause. "Miss Lyn? We aren't where you told me to go."

"I know, Luis, but you've been very kind, and this could be dangerous. I don't want you anywhere near what's about to happen." Reaching across the seat, past his shoulder, I startle him by flipping down the sun visor. "Are these your daughters?"

"*Sí*, they are." He almost looks embarrassed. But also proud.

I smile, for him, for them. "Then go back to them. And be happy. Take the money I gave you —"

"It's too much. I cannot —"

I cut him off. "Take it for now. If I can contact you... *after*... I will, and we can figure it all out. And if I can't contact you, well, I won't be needing the money back, anyway." I bark a laugh, trying to put him at ease with the crazy things I've just said.

"I will wait for you," he says. Luis is an admirable man.

"No," I say. "Not this time. Go home. If I can call you, I will."

Then Luis, a man I hardly know, takes my hand in his. "I think you are a good person, Miss Lyn. *Una bien pana*, as we say here. I very much wish to see you again, safely. Whatever you are doing, please be careful. I hope you get your *muérgano*, whoever he is." I'm not a hundred percent sure what Luis is saying, but he seems serious and seems to be rooting for me, and that's about all I can ask. I smile, nod, and say my goodbyes.

―――――

ONCE MORE, I'm sneaking toward a building. This one, however, is *much* different than any of the others. First of all, it's big. Long and tall, with a peaked roof, sitting just steps from the shore of Lake Maracaibo, with the city of Maracaibo — and the hotel with my nice, comfortable bed — looking back at me from the far side. At this distance, even the tallest buildings are tiny, like something built for ants. My only real connection to them seems to be the long line of General Urdaneta Bridge as it stretches across the water to my left.

Thick power lines droop down to the corner of the building from poles that run up the dirt driveway, and I loosely follow them to the side of the structure, feeling the building hum with energy. I'm not waiting around anymore. Not sneaking, or at least not much. Torden must know I'm coming for him anyway, given that Rand would have been incommunicado for some time now. Figuring it's the last thing he'd expect, I walk to the front door and pull it open with a loud metallic sound as it swings all the way out to bang against the exterior wall.

"I'm here!" I shout. "Show yourself!"

That feels pretty bold. Like, maybe *too* bold. The kind of overly bold thing someone says right before they get themselves killed. I hope that's not the case now.

Deflating the moment, there's no answer.

I close my eyes for a second, feeling with my EM power like I did when I took away Rand's, or when I boosted Percival's strength. Strangely, I feel nothing, no one near me. *God, am I on yet another wild goose chase?* But no, there's something else. The building... *It's full of electricity. The walls, the floor, the ceiling... It's — it's masking my ability to see anything clearly with my power in here.* Yeah, that seems an awful lot like something you'd do if you were, say, trying to trap an EM. I hesitate.

"Oh, just come inside, Ms. Hopkins. Stop being so dramatic," Torden's voice calls out with a slightly metallic tone, echoing from unseen loudspeakers. "I want you to see what I've created."

I stand on the threshold, unsure. I mean, there's no point in stealth now, he obviously knows exactly where I am, and I don't really have any intention of turning around and leaving without Percival. So I walk into the room and the door swings shut with a loud click behind me. You know, again like something you'd do if you were trying to trap someone. *Shit.*

The inside is dim, and my eyes work to adjust. Still, I put on an air of confidence that's only about a thousand magnitudes higher than I actually feel, and I call out. "Why are you hiding from me, Torden? Afraid to show your face?"

He laughs, tinny from the speakers. "On the contrary, my dear girl. I am... let's say, waiting for the right moment." His voice seems to come from everywhere, and I scan the huge space, noticing small black rectangular blocks high in several places. Next to each is a round object with a glowing red LED light in the lower center; he's got me well covered with cameras.

The room itself is massive and empty. Well, mostly empty. Along the walls, there are boxy metal markers spaced irregularly, some high, some low. Or perhaps they're targets. In other places, there are outlines of a loosely human form, with thick black bands hanging limply downward, which is more than a little bit creepy. *What is this place? A sort of shooting range? Torture chamber?*

The building itself is L-shaped, and from my position, I can only see about half of it — the lower section of the L, as I see it. I make my way to the bend, sliding up against the wall like some TV cop about to burst into a perp's apartment, then ease my way to the edge and peer around.

The other section of the building is closed off, with massive accordion doors from floor to ceiling. It reminds my vaguely of middle school gym class, where they'd use a similar type of collapsing wall to make multiple spaces out of one.

I know what's on the other side of the partition. I know who.

"Enough fooling around, Torden. It's time," I shout.

For a moment, there's nothing but silence. Then, I hear a loud click, and a gap appears in the wall ahead. Mechanical whirring grows louder as the wall folds slowly onto itself and its two sections retreat toward their separate sides.

On the loudspeakers, Torden chuckles, enjoying himself. "It *is* time, isn't it, Ms. Hopkins? I am *so* excited for you to see what I've done."

The room beyond seems as large as the room where I stand, but it has no windows. Its only illumination is the scant light from my end of the building, which is to say, not much light at all. I step out from the wall, placing myself directly in the middle of the long stretch of the building leading into that darkness.

Something at the far end glows faintly. No, not *glows*. Something is *lit* faintly, almost reverently.

I have a sudden memory of being twelve years old, forced to wear some fancy dress, and sitting on a hard bench beside my brother.

A pew.

A church.

We're in a church, and Kevin is in a suit. Sure, he often wears suits, but this one is all black. Not casual, but prim and... stiff. In my memory, I look up to see a long wooden casket of deep, dark mahogany. It's open, and inside, surrounded by silky white puffs, eyes closed and hands folded over her chest as if in prayer, is my Aunt Cindy. I remember she didn't look real. Not the way she looked in life. She almost looked like one of those wax figures they have in that tourist trap on 42nd Street in New York — realistic, sure, but something about the look triggers you to know they're fake. And something about them creeps under your skin and makes you certain, especially as a little kid, that they'll suddenly come to life, in all of their unnatural splendor, and rip you limb from limb.

But none of that is what triggers the memory. It's the thing behind Aunt Cindy's coffin... the cross.

I blink and refocus my eyes, and maybe the illumination at the far end of the large space grows, or maybe my eyes simply adjust. There, hanging high on the far wall, is a person. Arms spread, feet dangling, like a crucifixion. The person doesn't move, but even in low light I recognize him. How could I not?

"Percival!" I shout, rushing forward. I feel all at once like I can't breathe and my heart might burst. *Is he alive? Has Torden killed him and mounted him on the wall like some deer-head trophy? No!* Now that I'm in the same room, I rush forward and reach out with my EM senses, trying to detect him... And I find *two* sources, both deep wells. One is brimming with power while the other feels... empty. Empty, but not *gone*.

All at once, the lights in this new wing of the building pop on, a sudden and blinding brilliance that is brighter than the light of day outside. I stagger to a halt, shielding my eyes.

From somewhere ahead, a hear a slight whir and a loud, booming thud, followed closely by a repeat of those two sounds. I blink, looking into the bright space.

What I see defies understanding.

A machine... a robot? Some kind of man-shaped machine, lumbering toward me step by step, each one starting with that little mechanical spinning sound following by the bass boom of the footfall. I see exposed pistons and hoses, metal plates and gnarled hinges. And in the very middle, head poking up like kid in a Halloween costume, is the face of Torden Detonde.

"What in God's name...?"

He laughs. "Child, *God* had nothing to do with this."

Another step forward, and I realize this *thing*, this mechanical structure with Torden inside, isn't lumbering at all. It moves easily at his control; he doesn't seem the least bit strained by the effort. He smiles. Within the construct of the metal arms, I see Torden's arms, and his fingers flit lightly, followed immediately by the echoing movement of the massive metal hands that terminate each arm. "You've gone insane," I say, standing before him at my full height, which still means I'm dwarfed by the thing in front of me. Fear roils in the pit of my stomach. I expected to fight a powerful electromagician. Now I'm facing... what?

He's the size of one of those Mega Golems, the creatures he banded together from a hundred different parts of Stickmen. But he's not really like that — no clusters of hideous heads or grabbing hands. No, he's not a Mega Golem, he's something worse. Torden has turned himself into some sort of a *Mecha* Golem, and yeah, that name should be hilarious to me, because it's ridiculous, but I have the distinct feeling I'm about to learn everything his new creation can do, and a cold certainty that I won't like the experience.

"Do you like it, my machine?" he says, far too pleased with himself.

"Yeah, I do," I reply snidely. "I mean, most folks your age just go with a walker, but hey, you do you, Torden." He scowls, but I continue. "So *you* made *this* all by yourself?"

"Of course not! Don't be foolish, child."

"Then who helped? There's no one around anywhere, not here and not in that other place south of the city."

Torden chuckles. "Do you think I'm stupid enough to have my critical team of engineers and programmers just *hanging around* when I am about to deal with you?"

I try to wrap my head around that. *Torden has a team of engineers and programmers.* Then it dawns on me. The one thing I've always tried to ignore in my life, but the thing that speaks volumes to so many in this world. The thing that will have them bending over backwards, even for an insane old man like Torden: money. "You pay people, and they build what you want?"

"Basically," he says.

"Which means if someone were to pay them *more*..." Torden knows my family is rich. He understands my meaning.

"I pay my people quite well, and I can assure you that you won't be around long enough to meet even one of them." Torden's grin widens, full of insane ego.

"Oh, no, really, I think you should introduce us. I happen to know a *very* well qualified computer programmer of my own —" Kevin, of course. "— and I'm certain he'd be quite interested in what your *team* has been doing. It might even be, you know, the *touchstone* that begins a great friendship. Let me give him a call..." I pretend to reach into my pocket.

His smile falls. "Insufferably sarcastic to the last, eh, child? Well, soon this obnoxiousness you call *humor* will be the farthest thing from your mind. Once I begin the process."

"Process?" I ask. Something in my periphery moves, and I sneak a glance over Torden's massive metal shoulder to see Percival slowly writhing against the restraints holding him high on the wall. *He's alive*, I think, and my heart beats double-time. *He's really alive!* Though he looks like a man trying to come around after being drugged, the sight gives me renewed purpose. "I have a process for you, too, Torden. First, I kick your ass, then... well, then I just kill you. I'm done with giving you second chances."

The Mecha Golem freezes in place, almost unnaturally, as Torden bellows a hearty laugh. "Dear child, you have no idea what you're talking about. What you see before you, this *extension* of myself, is my greatest achievement. When I created my first golem — what you call a *Stickman* — I thought that was the ultimate; a creature I could loose on the world, able to suck up electromagic and feed it to me. Then I made the composite —" I can only assume he means the Mega Golem. "— and it was ten times as effective. But each required a source, an electromagician, or several, to act as the catalyst. So I developed my machine, the one you saw in Paris, to take power directly from one electromagician and give it to another. Still, it was big and bulky, and only worked in the place where I kept it. But now... Now I have *this*, and I can go *anywhere* and take any power, any time. Watch."

Suddenly, the right arm of the construct reaches forward with blinding speed, and I fall back into a defensive crouch. Something shoots from the metal palm of the thing, but it isn't aimed at me. It strikes one of the strange targets I saw on the walls earlier, and bursts into a tangle of electric arcs, blue-white flitting all over the tethered metal projectile like Torden is being electrocuted. Which, of course, he isn't. Just as quickly, his left arm thrusts out and another tentacle-like extension slams into a second target on that side. Both feed electricity into the main body of Torden's Mecha Golem. His face goes taut as the energy fills him.

But... if he's hitting targets along the wall, that's gotta be man-made electricity. All my life, I've been told that getting a charge that way is bad. Very bad. It turns you into an EM junkie, unable to do anything but stick your finger in a socket all day and night. "Am I supposed to be impressed? Now you're just a junkie."

Inside his power suit, Torden laughs again. "On the contrary, Lyn. I have developed a way to use *any* sort of power to fill me up, without the negative aspects our kind has experienced from generated electricity. Now, *any* source can charge me."

Well, shit. That's an unexpected development. And with me having not had a charge since... since when? Since before I even got to this country. I realize I'm in a bad spot. Still, I doubt what he's saying is one hundred percent true. Torden may be at least a partial junkie. The idea that he's willing to risk all that for power does not increase my confidence in his sanity. "You're out of your mind. How many other EMs have tried to use generated power? How many have failed?"

"And yet each of those that failed had one thing in common: *they* were not *me*."

"You're so arrogant. You think you can do no wrong. Well, I've got news for you, Torden. *Everything* you do is wrong. Making Stickmen and Mega Golems to suck the power out of other EMs. Doing your little experiments right under our noses, lying to everyone. Taking the lives of my friends. Killing..."

"Ah yes, killing. That's the main thing, right? The reason you've come? Revenge. So... *basic*."

My hands involuntarily ball into fists. "You killed my parents, you son of a bitch! Why?" I shout.

Torden shakes his head, not with guilt but with frustration. "Your parents called themselves Prime Order, yet how long did they plan to wait? How long before we take on the role we deserve? Regular humans are an *inferior* class of creature. Animals, really. We are stronger and we are better."

"That still doesn't explain it. You were at odds for years. What changed?"

Torden gestures to the metal construct around him. "*This*, Lyn. This is what changed. I made this, and now I know, it's time for *everything* to change. There's no more need to wait. In fact, I've wasted too much time already. And if it hadn't been for the way things happened between us, Lyn Hopkins, you and I might have been allies."

I nearly spit the awful taste that thought puts in my mouth. "Not if it were the last thing I ever do."

"No, not now. Of course." He nods with agreement, and it's as sinister as a nod can be. "Though of course, you yourself sought me as an ally, not that long ago."

"That was clearly a mistake. Don't you realize that — that you're the one who's wrong? You're broken and the things you do are *wrong*."

"Broken?" he repeats. "Well, perhaps, but it's no matter. If I am broken, then what are you? Fear me, if I am broken. Fear me, if I am whole. Fear me most of all, for now I am your *god*!"

No, you're not, and you'll never be. And I can do something about it. Something you're not expecting. I can take away your power forever and end this, right here and now. And so, I do.

I close my eyes and lean into my ability. I know from what happened with Rand that I can use Torden's own power against him, but Percival is nearby, too. Between the two, I should have no trouble juicing up. Simultaneously, I reach out and pull in, tugging at both sources of EM power in the room and mentally twisting them together, then driving that into Torden like an invisible syringe, intent on sucking whatever it is inside him that makes him like me. Turning it off for good. For a moment, I feel the process flowing, feel him diminishing.

I open my eyes and see the startled look in Torden's eyes. He's so stunned, he's let the two projectile appendages drop to the floor with a double thud, and he glares back at me wide-eyed. I see the fear. It propels me, and I double my efforts.

Then Torden blinks. His right hand slips free of the grip used to control that mechanical arm and reaches for a set of buttons and knobs mounted on his chest. He flicks one, turns another... and my efforts are immediately blocked, suddenly as useless as trying to squeeze blood from a stone.

"*That*," Torden says in a breathy, almost rapturous voice. "That was quite an unexpected surprise, Lyn Hopkins." He smiles with unbridled amazement until the corners of his eyes squint and his grin turns into a sneer. "And I shall be thrilled to take *that* ability from you along with all the others. You're really proving to be quite the treasure trove. Thank you so much for coming to me and making this easy." Slipping his hand back into the construct's arm controls, he does something that causes the two tentacles to retract back into his metal hands. "Now, to begin, I will drain your power. Once that's done, it will be such a pleasure to pluck your special capabilities from you, one by one."

"Why didn't it work?" I ask in a low voice to myself.

But Torden hears me. "My girl, did you think I built a power suit that would allow power *out*? Of course not." He laughs. Then, tilting his head in with an almost fatherly look of admiration, Torden points both of his metal palms directly at me, and fires his tethered projectiles at my body, one hitting me high on the left, near my collarbone, and the other low on my stomach, near my right hip bone. They burrow into my flesh even as I'm staggered backward until the tentacles reach their lengths and halt my fall. They lift me up, helpless, off the ground, with some sort of electrodes now stuck in me like the tines of a fork. Then, as if syphoning gas through a tube, his machine delves to the depths of my well of power, seeking the entirety of my Quotient, being the process of draining every ounce of electromagic from my body.

33

THE NEVER-ENDING STORM OF CATATUMBO

I'm drained. I feel completely weak. The electrodes unplug themselves from my body, leaving my shirt dotted with red circles of blood where the metal bits stabbed into me. But that pain is nothing. I feel nothing. Because what's inside of me... is nothing.

I stagger forward, nearly falling on my face but somehow able to end up on hands and knees. I tilt my head up to look at the monstrous machine that Torden has become, and I see his face.

His mouth hangs open, his eyes are closed. The entire metal construct around him appears limp.

He looks like a man in the throes of ecstasy.

I realize I have only a few seconds to act.

I push myself up to stand, but I'm so exhausted that my back bends and I wonder if I can even walk. Still, I try. I turn my back on Torden's Mecha Golem and shuffle away, toward the door I came in. *God, I hope it's not locked.*

With every step, I'm sure that Torden will notice, will send one of those tentacles flying toward me and stab me with electrodes once again. I dare to glance back, just once, and see him there still, deep in the throes of joy from what he's taken. Well, he did take all of my power, and given my supposed Quotient, maybe that was quite the charge. I only hope it gives me enough time to get out of here, to make a new plan somehow.

I reach the door and push.

Nothing. It's locked. *Damn it.*

I push again, but it's futile, so then I start to look around frantically. There's a square button to one side, like the ones I saw at his other installation. Could it be that simple? I push it and hear an electric hum and a click. Skeptical, I lean into the door once more, and almost fall out onto the dirt when the thing opens easily.

I'm outside, and Torden hasn't moved yet.

Now what?

I'm not thinking that far ahead. I just want to get *out.* I scan the area. It's growing dark already, which seems odd. It can't be that late in the day yet, can it?

Then I see flashes reflected on the wide waters of Lake Maracaibo. Flashes in the sky. *Lightning.* I stagger forward, still so empty, so spent.

The shoreline is only a few meters away, but so what? What am I going to do when I get there? Go for a swim?

Behind me, there's a loud mechanical whir as a huge bay door glides upward. Standing in the opening is Torden within his massive robotic power suit. He strides out into the clearing with ease. "You can't get away, child," he says with a smug laugh.

Above us, heat lightning skitters through the clouds, each one echoed by its reflection on the surface of the water. But how can I get there, so high in the sky?

I reach deep inside myself, looking for any power, anything that will let me glow and fly, just for a moment —

One of Torden's metal tentacles batters into my back, sending me sprawling into the dirt face first. The electrode within it extends and prods a new hole in my flesh, and I shriek in pain. Then the second tentacle strikes, pushing me down with renewed force. Once it digs its metal latches into me, they both start to retract, dragging me through rocks and leaves and sticks and mud, back toward *him.* I claw at the dirt, trying to resist, but it's useless. After I moment, I give up that futile fight.

This is the end.

The end.

And once I'm dead, he'll do the same to Percival. Pers was just bait to get me here. And it worked. I didn't save him, and I got myself killed, too.

All I feel is pain. The minor, undignified pain of being scraped along the ground, but mostly the deep, violated feeling of Torden's metal electrodes buried in my skin. I feel them. I feel them.

And I realize what else I feel.

Him.

The metal prongs sticking into me are a conduit. From me, my EM power, back to Torden. Maybe not directly to him, but to whatever battery or storage cell his Mecha Golem construct has to sap my electricity.

It's *connected*.

As suddenly as they struck, the two tentacles detach from my body and slip back into their housing in Torden's mechanical arms. He looks to the sky. "Do you see that above you, Lyn? Do you know what that is?"

I roll over onto my back in the dirt, face to the sky, spitting grit out of my mouth. "Lightning," I stammer. *Do I feel different?*

"Yes, of course. Our old friend lightning. You used to call yourself that. *Lightning* Hopkins. Rather arrogant for one of our kind, don't you think? To co-opt the thing that gives us all our charge and make it a name for only *you*. But do you know what's special about *this* lightning, child?" He stands there, face looking small within the metal body surrounding it, gazing happily at the flashes in the clouds.

"I have no idea what you're talking about," I say. *I feel different. I do.*

Torden casually raises his hands, and the mechanical arms glide upward with ease. Then the two tentacles fire outward, into the sky, and go rigid. He stands there, making a giant letter Y, and as if he calls it forward, a bolt of lightning breaks from the clouds, forks in midair, and strikes the electrode ends of both tentacles. "This!" he shouts over the deafening clack of the air collapsing back into the space where the lightning struck. "This is the Never-Ending Storm of Catatumbo! Here at Lake Maracaibo, there are more lightning strikes than any other place on earth. Here! The perfect place for me to build and test my ultimate creation." Again, as if he is calling it by will, lightning strikes those tentacle arms again. I press my hands hard against my ears as the world shakes from the crackling sound of thunder.

But I feel different. I really do. When Torden's electrodes were stuck in me, I could feel his well of power. I could tap into it. And just before they disconnected from my body, I could steal some, too.

I stand up, defiantly.

"That sound," I say, gesturing to the echo now fading. "That's all you are, Torden Detonde."

"What are you talking about, little girl?" he chides.

"Thunder. You are nothing but the useless noise of thunder." And without warning, I fill myself with that little bit of power I stole and burst skyward, toward those beautifully electric clouds.

I glance down, watching Torden recede. With amazingly fast reflexes, he thrusts his tentacles upward to stop me, but they can only extend so far and in a millisecond, I'm out of reach. He seems to be trying to fly himself, but can't get off the ground. *The product of being strapped into a heavy metal suit, I bet. Jackass.* I even dare a smile.

A moment later, I plunge into the billowy and thick grey clouds, and instantaneously I'm struck by the first bolt of lightning.

It's a joy I can't describe.

Another strike, and another.

I don't just *accept* the charge they give me; I *pull* on each one, tapping them dry.

Another and another, and now I realize I'm demanding the lightning to strike me. I'm calling the power to me.

The space around me blazes in blinding blue-white as a ball of pure electric power forms. I'm holding my arms out, almost how I saw Percival, strapped to the wall in a sort of crucifixion, though I'm not being tortured or punished.

I'm becoming one with the power of the storm. *Catatumbo*, as

Torden called it. The never-ending storm. I reach out and pull all of it into me, until I feel like I might burst. I've charged countless times in my life, but nothing compares — not the greatest tornado or even the superbolt Percival and I took in France. *Nothing.*

I spin and spin, lightning striking every part of my body, and all of it sucked down into my deep well. All the power of the never-ending storm fills me.

I'm glowing — no, that's not right. I'm lit like the sun, so full of white hot energy. Finally, something tells me the process is complete, and I let myself fall back to earth. I slowly descend out of the clouds, to the same place where Torden stands waiting. Gently, I touch down right in front of him.

He grins, but his eyes are unnaturally wide. "I knew you'd return. We have unfinished business, you and I."

"Things are different now, Torden." The white ball of light around me casts his shadow onto the large building behind him and washes out the nearby landscape.

"No," he says with a shrug. "They really aren't. You have filled yourself up, but I will simply drain you again. Just as I could do it a thousand more times." Quicker than I can move out of the way, the tentacles once more strike me and dig their electrodes into my skin. How many bleeding holes do I have now? I've lost count.

I go to tap my power, to fight back, and realize I can't. Even with all the electromagic within me, something about being connected to Torden this way deadens my abilities.

No! This can't be happening! I got charged!

But it is. I drop to my knees in the dirt, dejected. Feeling the overwhelming amount of power within me drain away for the second time in just a few moments.

As if its laughing at me, the Never-Ending Storm of Catatumbo lives up to its name, with lightning zigging and zagging across the sky, like my time up there filling myself with electromagic power meant as little to the storm as it now does to Torden.

Helpless to stop it, I feel the electricity flowing out of my body as Torden Detonde stares down at me with a pitiless air of victory.

34

AT LAST YOU ARE FREE

The sheer stupidity of my defeat pisses me off.

It's embarrassing.

I mean, if I have to fail, if I have to die, can't there be some shred of dignity to it all? Do I have to lose everything with some dopey *whoopsy* face on?

Damn it.

I mean that. *Damn it.*

Fine. If you want all of my electromagic and all my abilities, Torden, take them! Take every last bit!

Instead of resisting, I give up and *push*.

Finally, I'll be free of all this. Take everything, you son of a bitch!

Push!

Something tickles my nose.

I try to force my power into the electrodes connecting me to Torden's power suit. Every drop of energy I have, funneled down to those tiny points, those little receptors.

Push!

I smell something, an acrid smell.

Looking down, where the tentacles are plugged into opposite sides of my stomach, I notice tiny tendrils of smoke. Almost simultaneously, Torden sees the problem. I feel the electrodes retract as he tries to break the connection, but I won't let that happen. I grab the two metal prods and hug them against me, and with renewed effort I push my electromagic into them, sending more energy than I've ever held before up the wires and into Torden's power suit.

"Stop it! Damn you, girl!" his voice sounds distant, frantic.

I feel it when the wires start to burn. It feels good.

I push harder. *You made a suit that won't let power out? Well, let me make sure plenty of power gets in.*

The smell intensifies as some part of Torden's construct starts to melt. He pulls away, but I keep holding on, and all he succeeds in doing is dragging me across the dusty ground. Rocks scrape at my knees, but I won't let him go. I force my power into the electrodes, up the tentacles and into Torden himself.

Now there's smoke inside the suit, puffing out around his neck, flowing into his hair. His face tells me everything: Torden Detonde is terrified and doesn't know what to do. "Stop it! Now!"

"No," I say calmly, still pushing, pushing, pushing. "I told you you're nothing, Torden. Just the empty sound of thunder. But me? *I am lightning.*"

At that, the wires in his tentacles finally fail, bursting into flame and falling away. No matter. I send bolts of white-hot energy into the two sockets on his metal hands, blasting it with more electricity than I knew I could even control.

The Never-Ending Storm has filled me with power, and now I am filling Torden's mechanical construct with it, overloading it. The thing he built to suck up EM power and protect him has become a prison. Torden is stuck in his own failing device, unable to escape as I burn through all of it, burn it all away, down to the man himself.

I've always been told that electromagicians can't hurt each other with their magic, but I've never tried it like this before. Sending so *much* power into another that they simply can't handle it.

Like the way we overloaded the Stickmen. Like overloading a circuit. Torden's construct is man-made, and that means it has a limit.

Just then, I feel the moment when Torden's suit gives out.

Suddenly, I can feel my energy going straight into him, not his unnatural metal robot shell. I stand up, focusing my efforts on this man who has taken so much from me.

He struggles, but at first he can take it... if only for a moment. Unfortunately for Torden, he's already brimming with power from using his suit to suck it out of the sockets on the walls of his weird testing lab, and from the lightning strikes, and from bleeding me dry the first time around. That means there's really nowhere for all of my considerable energy to go.

As I watch, it's no longer the power suit that burns, it's Torden himself. His skin darkens and chars, his hair smolders and falls out in black clumps, and his eye sockets grow deep. "I have been alive for over two *hundred* years, you indignant child!"

"All things must end," I say as I pulse one last, massive burst of electromagic into him.

Trapped inside his metal husk, Torden burns until only his bones are left. Until there is only the charred remains of the man who has taken so much from me and from the ones I love.

As I release the flow of electricity, the sudden vacuum of power causes the entire metal construct to fall forward, burying what's left of Torden Detonde face down in the dirt. *Good. I was sick of looking at him, anyway.*

For a moment, all is still.

Torden Detonde is dead, a man kept alive long past any reasonable life span, simply because he stole the lives of others. *How many?*

Then I see something move. Coming out of the suit. Torden? Still alive? Impossible.

No, it isn't Torden, but it is human-shaped. A man, someone I don't know, rises up. His form is clear, but not solid. I can see through him in places, like he's a ghost. Or a memory. He looks at me and gives me a nod, then fizzles away into nothingness, dust on a passing gust of wind.

"What the—?" But before I can even rationalize what I just saw, there's another form. This time a woman. Really more like vapors in the form of a woman, but she too nods at me before dissipating.

Then another, and another. Young, old, male, female.

"Are you?" I don't even want to say it out loud, but I have to. "Are you the ones he killed? To make himself live longer?"

None of them speak. But they each nod at me, a sign of thanks.

So many, I can't even count. Dozens. Hundreds?

Then one of them lingers, just a little bit longer than the ones before, and I realize I know the face. "Hayden." As I say his name, he nods like the others, and I start to cry. "Oh God, you've all been stuck inside this monster..."

The wispy form of Hayden grows amorphous and seems to puff into a cloud, soon taken by a swirl of air and gone forever. A moment later, I see my old friend, Zeb, Uma's brother. He nods and fades away like all the others before him.

Then there is another.

Right away, I recognize him. *Oh, I wish Zee were here to see this.* "Robin... I've missed you so much. She has, too, Robin. Zee loves you." Still, there are no words, just a nod. But his face. Those eyes. I can see he hears me. But nothing holds him in place, not anymore. The ghostly form of my old friend loses definition and, like the others, floats away into the air.

More come, many more. All I can do is watch, crying at so many lives lost. So many Torden took, just for his own gain.

What would Torden have done if I had failed? If he had been able to take my abilities? I can make EMs. I can unmake EMs.

My abilities aren't natural, and I don't know what to do about that. But at least they didn't end up in his hands. Whatever I might think is wrong with me, for having these powers, at least I know I won't be like *him*.

I'd rather die than use my powers to hurt innocent people. To take from them and give it all to me? No. I'd rather die than do that.

Finally, the last of the ghosts follows the others on the wind, rising over Lake Maracaibo and disappearing like a puff of smoke. Or maybe they've all reached the clouds and become one with the Never-Ending Storm of Catatumbo. *Yes, yes, I hope so.* I stand there a long time, looking out over the water. I'm not even sure how long.

———

EVENTUALLY, I hear footsteps approaching, and I turn around to see Orkan Zidane, wearing a finely tailored grey suit, walking up with a group of armed men. The men quickly form a protective perimeter, as Orkan looks down at the bizarre sight of Torden's charred metal construct. "Is he... inside that?"

"Yes," I say flatly.

"And he's —"

"Dead. Absolutely."

"Then I guess we arrived too late to be of much help," Orkan says.

"How is it that you're even here?" I realize that the last time I saw Orkan was when I freed him from the Bissets in Paris.

"You saved my life. I thought I might try to repay the favor, so I called your brother and he told me you were looking for Torden in Maracaibo. I didn't know exactly where until you put on that show in the clouds."

"Show?"

"This place is known for its lightning storms, but what I saw was clearly unnatural. I figured it had to be you, up high in the clouds, drawing all those strikes to you. Then it was just a matter of trying to get here as fast as we could. What is this thing anyway?" Orkan gestures toward the smoldering metal.

"Torden thought it was a good idea to build a mechanical suit to suck up all the electricity he could."

"And what did you do?"

"I gave him what he wanted. Every ounce of my power, all at once."

Orkan's eyebrows rise and he stares at me. "Remind me not to get on your bad side."

35

AND THE WALLS CAME DOWN

There's a click just before it happens.

Neither one of us sees it coming.

And I'm not fast enough to save him.

The gunshots are so close that the sound is deafening, and I turn away like a reflexive action. Something else happens, too: instinctively, I form a ball of electromagic around me like a shield. I hear the pinging sounds of ricochets as bullets bounce off it.

But Orkan is too far away. I can't get to him, fold him into my shield, before it's too late. His body jerks as red blotches appear on his fine grey suit. Stains that won't ever come out. I truly believe he's dead before his body hits the ground.

I turn toward the gunmen, furious, still holding onto my sphere of protection. "Why?" It's all I can think to ask. "Don't you *work* for him?"

"We used to," one of the men says, a burly guy with black and grey stubble on a chin that looks like it was chiseled out of granite. "But we go with the best odds these days."

"The best *odds*? What the hell does that even mean?" I keep my shield powered up, because frankly I don't trust these guys at all.

"We represent the interests of Torden Detonde now," the man says, as if that explains anything.

I point at the burnt metal thing on the ground. "He's *dead*, you idiots! That's Torden Detonde right there!"

Clearly they don't believe me, because the one who's speaking gestures to the others, and several of them combine their efforts and manage to roll over the big metal form of Torden's Mecha Golem. Not that it matters much. What remains of Torden within the structure is nothing more than charred bones. I guess they're going to have to take my word on it.

"Doesn't matter. We were to arrive at Torden's location, then execute Plan 7."

"And what is that, anyway? Running around, shooting people? For what?"

The square-chinned man lowers the muzzle of his weapon toward the ground. "There's a reckoning coming for electromagicians. Even you have to see that. We intend to be on the right side when the war comes."

War? A war is coming? I had thought the death of Torden might bring some kind of normalcy back to the world, some kind of peace for me. Maybe I was very, very wrong about that.

The armed men turn and begin to walk off, and I realize that I should probably do something. *What? Kill them? Shoot them in the back with a bolt of lightning? No. No, that's not something I'm prepared to do.*

Instead, I just let them go.

———

"ABOUT TIME. I thought you were just gonna leave me up here." So Percival is alive and at least well enough to manage sarcasm. I don't see a ladder or anything else to climb on to get up to where he's strapped to the wall, so instead I fill myself with power — amazed to find out how much I still have in me — and float up to him.

In contrast, Percival has virtually no charge, and has to hold on to me tightly to avoid plummeting to the hard floor below. Having his arms wrapped around me, even though it's out of necessity, feels... good.

His face inches away, Pers looks tired. Spent. "Are you okay?" I ask tentatively.

"Yeah, but I could really use a charge."

As if in answer, I see flickers of light from outside. *Well, it is a never-ending storm, supposedly.* "I think I know where you can find one." Without EM power, I could never lift him, but flowing with energy, the act is trivial. So instead of gently floating him down to the ground, I fly with him out the large bay door and up, up into the clouds brimming with so much electricity.

Together, high above Lake Maracaibo, Percival and I are struck over and over by the seemingly endless lightning these incredible clouds produce. In short order, Pers is fully charged, and I've pulled in so much power that I wonder if my body is even storing it anymore. For the first time in my life, I think I'm being struck by lightning for no reason whatsoever. It's a tremendously weird feeling.

Once Pers has enough juice, he floats among the clouds using his own EM abilities, and I find myself saddened when we aren't touching anymore.

After a time, we drift back down to the ground. The sky has darkened, so maybe we weren't seen, but I'm past caring, really.

"You wanna tell me what happened?" Pers asks.

"Not really. Later."

"You killed him, though, right?"

"Yeah," I say. "And afterward, something happened. The EMs he killed were, I don't know... released? That sounds about right. I saw them, our friends."

"Hayden? Zeb? And... wow, even Robin?"

I nod, but tears are in the corners of my eyes again, so I say nothing.

I don't know why we came back to the same place, but we did. Orkan's body lies in a bloody heap next to the weird robotic creation that envelops Torden Detonde's blackened bones. "What happened to Orkan?"

"His own guards turned on him, shot him dead."

"That seems... bad."

"Yeah, bad for all of us. They said a war is coming."

"What does that mean?" Pers asks. "A war between *us* and *them*, between EMs and regulars?"

"I hope not. But I don't know." *Probably. And that's the worst thing for all of us.*

We stand there for some time in silence, and then Percival comes closer and wraps his arms around me. Despite it all, despite standing so close to death, if I could make time stand still, this moment would never end.

36

HIGH TIME TO GET TO SEA

I'm charge hunting again, off in the plains of America's Midwest. It's like old times.

And yet, it's not.

For as long as I can recall, or at least as long as I've been old enough to travel on my own, these excursions have been absolutely and strictly *solo* affairs.

I know. Everyone always got mad at me for running off by myself, but I had to have time not only to recharge with electricity, but also to simple *recharge*. And for someone like me, that means being *alone*.

There's a knock on the door, but I set an alarm on my phone and woke to its gentle buzzing beside my head. I've been getting dressed in the dark for eight minutes or so, meaning I'm already ready.

I quietly unlock and open the motel door to find Zee, my best friend in all the world, smiling at me. Such a best friend that she didn't abandon me, despite what I did to her back when we were kids. She just needed time to wrap her head around it all. "Shall we?" she says, jauntily extending one bent elbow with a smile. Her well-worn jeans are tucked into hiking boots, and behind her I see the sky roiling with angry clouds, just the thing for people like us.

"We shall," I say, grinning and taking her arm as I step out. The room behind me is dark, but the light from outside is just enough to illuminate the mop of blond curls poking out from the comforter on the queen sized bed.

From somewhere in that direction, we hear a yawning groan. "Again?" Pers says, slowly sitting up and blinking from the light. As he stretches, the blankets fall down to show his bare chest.

Mackenzie turns away in false embarrassment. "My eyes," she says, but I know she's kidding.

"Come on," I say, stepping out of the room. "Let's let Prince Charming rest."

"Hey!" Pers says indignantly. "Did you turn off my alarm?"

I stifle a laugh at the comment, and Zee giggles beside me. "Maybe? I figured you could use the extra sleep. You know, after last night..."

"Lyn Hopkins!" Zee says, mouth agape. "Are you implying something?"

"Oh, I'm not implying anything. I'm saying it right out. Come on, let's go." I pull the door closed behind me, leaving Percival once more in the dark.

Zee and I cross the parking lot, hearing the muffled noises of Pers falling out of bed behind us. He shouts something, but the motel walls are surprisingly good at blocking the sound. Given that Zee's room is next door, and given the, um, raucous nature of the previous night, that's probably a good thing.

We reach the far side and step into the grass, which in turn leads to the tree line, which then leads up the hill. Rain starts to fall. A front is moving in, and there will be storms. We just have to be mobile enough to catch them.

I think back to Maracaibo. Whatever charge I get today will be nothing in comparison. You'd think someone like me would make Venezuela a regular destination, but I may be done with South America after what I've been through, no offense to the millions of people who live there.

I freeze, and a moment later, so does Zee. "What's wrong?" she asks.

"This," I say. "This isn't my normal routine. It's... *weird* to have you both here with me."

"Lyn Hopkins, you've run away from us for almost ten years, whenever you feel like you need a little space. It's about time you let your friends help you."

"I guess you're right." I laugh.

"What's so funny?" Zee asks.

I look at her sideways. "I sort of feel bad for leaving Pers behind."

"No, you don't," she says immediately.

I laugh again. "Okay, you got me. I don't." We keep hiking up the hill.

Somewhere below us, the door to my motel room opens and Pers stumbles out. "Wait up, you guys!" he calls from a distance.

I've told Zee, of course. Told her about Robin's spirit leaving Torden's body. She took it as well as someone could, I suppose, but that's a night neither of us will ever remember, because it involved a rather obscene amount of tequila.

And I've realized something. These people matter to me, more than anything else. They're important.

I have some kind of strange gift, my abilities, things other EMs can't do. Right now, I feel that being an EM is pretty much a liability. No one's gone public with us, not yet, but everything is tense and the war that I was warned of seems close at hand. I have no idea what will happen when the whole world knows we exist, and we have to fight not to be wiped out of existence. I never asked for any of this.

But I spent 20 years without parents, because they were worried what my special powers could do. I've worried about it myself. Now, it's time to stop worrying.

To live life.

With the ones I love.

I spent so much time trying to avoid pain and heartache, but that was all I got, anyway. Now, I'm going to revel in the time I have with these people. Zee's even started dating. He's a nice guy, I think. Orlando is his name, and even though she didn't feel the time was right to bring him on this trip, it may be soon. I'm happy she's happy.

And Percival.

When I thought Torden might have killed him, I nearly died. Now that I have him back in my arms, I'll do anything to keep it that way.

And, if in time we have kids, I suspect they might be electromagicians, just as Kevin and I were a product of our two EM parents.

I won't run, even if they have abilities I can't understand. I won't.

I'm still trying to love my parents, even though I disagree with how they left me. They made a choice.

I would have made a different choice, but that's how it worked out. I don't know if it's a good thing that we spent their final 24 hours together, or if that makes everything worse. I want to hope it was some saving grace.

Torden is gone, but like-minded people live on. People I don't know, and even my brother Kevin and his seemingly endless technical chops can't put names to them, not yet.

War is on the horizon.

But I will spend however much time I have before that war, and I will live and love and be with the people that matter.

The clouds above rumble with thunder and Zee's face lights up.

Yes, I think. *The most normal of things to do, to be with friends, and to smile and laugh.*

Ever been struck by lightning? I know I have. And once more it happens, as the beautiful forked tongue of the cloud dragon stabs into me again.

But it's not the charge that's making me smile. It's the face of my friend, Zee, beside me like old times.

THE END

of

THUNDER

Lightning Hopkins
Book 3

NEWSLETTER

ABOUT THE AUTHOR

Keith Soares

For 22 years, Keith Soares ran an interactive game, web, and app development agency working with clients like National Geographic, PBS, Verizon, HarperCollins, and the Smithsonian Institution. As a team leader dealing with agency deadlines and late nights waiting on code updates, he converted some of the inevitable downtime into creative time and started writing science fiction and fantasy novels in 2013.

In 2020, Keith left the agency world behind to become a full-time author, trading computer code for plot outlines. He lives in Alexandria, Virginia, with his wife and two daughters, who are all avid readers.

If you've enjoyed this book, I hope you'll consider leaving a very brief review with the store where you purchased it. Thanks.